Johnny Lazarus in Wave of Courage

Written and Illustrated by
Keith Poletiek

RYLEE —
GOD BLESS!
Keith Poletiek

Wide Open PRODUCTIONS

THanKS!

THanKS continue to go out
to my overly supportive
family, Tina, Noah
Myranda & Abella
THanKS also, once again,
to all the guys at
WideOpen Productions
"Johnny Lives" because
of your talents!
THanKS to my mom, Pat,
for all the help in making
this possible!
THanKS again to
Robin Blumenthal for
great editing and insight!
THanKS Timmer the Swimmer
for always challenging me!
THanK YOU Jesus
THanK YOU Lord!

Congratulations to Laurie Dorr -
The Unique Word Contest
Winner for:
"alluvium" (pg 11)

Table of Contents

aUTHOR'S nOTe

cOURaGe.

The Dictionary defines courage as: *the quality that enables a person to face difficulty, danger, pain, etc., without fear.*

I often wonder if people look at me and think of me as a courageous person. If they do, then I've fooled them for sure, because deep down inside of me, I'm not. Not by nature anyway. I too, may roar on the outside, but just like the Cowardly Lion in the Wizard of Oz, I could use a bit of, *"What put the ape in apricot . . . Courage!"*

In this great adventure, *Wave of Courage*, Johnny is going to be faced with difficulty, danger, pain, etc. The question is, can he face it without fear? Can he muster up enough courage to take on life's challenges and win?

If I told you the answer to these questions, I'd be giving away the ending to the book, so you'll have to dig down deep and find the courage to read on!

Johnny will face another kind of courage in this adventure as well. One that is even more important for him and those around him. The courage to stick to his convictions and be willing to feel a "Wave of Courage" come over him that is so strong, he feels compelled to share his convictions with the people he cares about, because the truth behind his convictions are life-changing!

Will Johnny find this "Wave of Courage?"

Again, nice try, but you'll just have to gather up some courage and dive into "Johnny Lazarus in Wave of Courage" to find out!...Surf's up!

JOHNNY'S SURF FACT NO. 1
Huntington Beach, CA has such a great surfing history that it adopted the name "Surf City USA"

CHAPTER ONE:
"WHAT AM I DOING HERE?"

"Totally mega-awesome!"
Those were the only words that came out of my mouth as I stared at the most amazing sight I had ever seen in my life. I was frozen on the sand, unable to move, like a deer caught in the headlights of an oncoming car. Trouble was moving my way, big trouble, but I didn't leap out of the way. I just stood there with my mouth hanging open, mesmerized by its' amazing power. Not a smart move; or non-move in this case.

Dad said I wasn't always the sharpest tool in the shed and this time I was like a saw that couldn't cut through butter. Melted butter!

Usually, a bike ride to the beach meant putting on my wetsuit, grabbing my board and attacking the waves for a great day of surfing, but not today. There would be no attacking *these* waves; not this time. I knew if I or any other fool dared try, these waves would win and win *big*!

I could only stand in awe and ask myself over and over again, "What am I doing here?"

"Awesome! Amazing! Cool!" I was having a hard time describing these monsters of the sea because they weren't normal, at least not normal for the waves that usually rolled up on the beach here in my hometown. Our waves didn't scare me or make me stop and stare, not anymore anyway, but these mega-daddies did! In fact, these bad boys would make most surfers, in most parts of the world stop and stare because these babies were huge! Fifteen to twenty feet high easy! Maybe even higher!

They were so big that they caused some people to panic when they pounded on the shore.

"Run for your life!" some guy yelled as he ran passed me.

A twenty, maybe twenty-five footer, was getting too close for his liking.

I didn't run though. I just stood there trying to decide if I was a safe enough distance away from its furry. I took three steps back just in case, maybe four!

As the wave creped slowly towards me I could sense it staring at me. I could feel it wanting to reach out and grab me; we all could. I began to quiver a bit but kept my nerve. The guy next to me took off running like a bank robber who had just heard the siren of a police car approaching.

I found myself sizing up the wave instead.

"What was I thinking?"

It was a twenty foot, mammoth wall of bluish-green water, the likes of which I or anyone else from around here had never seen. It was the biggest and most ferocious beast to invade our shores ever and this *dude* was just one in a day-long assault of these huge water monsters. It was both impressive and unnerving all at the same time.

They even rivaled some of the big waves featured in some of the surfing magazines I had looked through over the years. Pipeline or the North Shore in Hawaii had nothing on these monsters. These waves were bigger and more powerful than anyone could have imagined.

I had grown up at this beach and I had seen some pretty

big waves over the years, but none of them even came close to these. This was nature at its finest and I knew I was standing in the very presence of God's mighty power!

There it was. That question that kept popping up in my head over and over, "What am I doing here?"

There were only a handful of us standing close to the waves now. Most people had been chased back by the lifeguards for fear of injury or even getting snagged by one of these behemoths and dragged out to sea.

The beach was closed for miles in both directions, north and south, and for good reason; because there wasn't really much beach left to speak of. It was gone; or at least gone from sight.

The waves crashed down on the sand with such force that water was now rushing up and swallowing the sand where the beach *used to be.*

Sea water washed in, time and time again, soaking the area where people would usually set up their chairs, umbrellas and towels to enjoy the day. Now, only a swirled mess of wet sand, an alluvium of mud and debris, was left where white sand once gleamed. Dude, it was nasty!

And you can forget about the fire rings used for cooking hot dogs, or toasting marshmallows for making s'mores.

Don't you love a good s'more? I love watching the gooey marshmallow and chocolate come together inside the cracker. The smell itself made your mouth water. Ummm! So good!

"Boom!" The sound of the wave crashing down woke me from my marshmallow fantasy. I must have been hungry.

Anyway, the fire rings were nowhere to be found. These

waves even had the strength to send water racing all the way to the boardwalk that neared the street. This walking and biking path was usually well removed from harm's way, but not today. On any other day it was at least a thousand feet from a normal high tide, but today that thousand foot safety cushion was gone; swallowed whole by relentless water that kept pushing its way onto the shore.

Whether invited or not, these waves were crashing the party, and for most of us, they came unannounced. How rude!

The pier, with its tall, watchful lifeguard tower, had for years been an icon in our town. It stood above the ocean below and announced with its presence that everyone in her shadow could feel safe. The lifeguards that inhabited her kept their eye on everything that moved in the water below and you could almost feel their eyes on you as you swam or surfed. It was a good feeling.

But now that same tower, and the pier itself, looked dwarfed by the walls of water coming in, and it too was taking a massive beating from the continued waves pounding against her. They even closed the pier to foot traffic due to the danger.

I moved forward a bit, looking for a great location to take pictures of all that was happening. I knew that no one was ever going to believe what I was seeing without proof. I knew that someday, when I was older, like next month, I'd try and describe to Henry or Richie or even Summer what I saw and they would, or at least Henry and Richie would say, "Yeah, Right!" So I brought my trusty camera with me and recorded, picture after amazing picture, this event to end all events happening in our little beach community.

Speaking of Henry and Richie; "Where were they?"

Why weren't they here with me? My two amigos were missing the greatest day in our beach's history! My camera wasn't doing justice to what was really taking place here. This was a you-had-to-see-it-to-believe-it moment and they were nowhere to be found. We lived for these kinds of moments. We had so many stories of great times in our past. All one of us would have to do is say words like "Turner's Farm" or a name like "Coastal Eddie" and the stories and laughs would fly. We were all first class storytellers and every time we got together we would all try to outdo each other with how wild we could make a story turn out.

Well, here was a story that didn't need any pumping up to seem outrageous; it was outrageous, and they were missing it!

News vans had started to arrive. Police were beginning to block off sections of the coastal highway. Helicopters were now circling in the air. This was an event. A full-blown, watch the six o'clock news event and I was right here in the middle of it.

The question still remained, "What am I doing here?"

I watched in amazement as lifeguards chased surfers from the beach.

"What were those guys thinking?" And yet, I knew.

They were thinking what every hardcore surfer watching this on television was thinking.

"I wish I was there, man! I'd ride one of those bad boys all the way to the donut shop across the street!"

Which was now feasible because the waves were growing bigger and bigger.

I watched as a wave washed up past me and plowed into the sandbags that were now being filled and placed in front of the beach shops that lined the street across from the pier. These were prime spots to have your shop because of all the beach traffic and tourists that walked by, especially in the summer. I snapped a picture of that!

I was then startled by a loud, "Whoa!" from the crowd of people around me and I turned quickly to see what was causing all the commotion. It was another wave, but this one was even bigger than any that had come before it, and to all of our amazement, when it crashed into the pylons of the pier, it sent white water so high into the air that sea water actually splashed on to the pier itself. That had to be about fifty feet in the air easy! Then the wave after that did the same thing and on and on. These were bigger than twenty-footers. They just had to be!

I had to get a picture of this! Maybe just to convince myself later that this was really happening! I moved quickly to my right, holding my camera up to my eye, watching intently for the next wave to come. I wanted to get a picture of the wave right at the point of impact with the pier and show how incredibly high the white wash was soaring. It was defying gravity!

Here's a good question, "What am I doing here?"

As I moved to my right, with my camera perched on my eye, I ran into something that stopped me in my tracks. The camera slammed into my cheek and I shouted, "Ow!"

All my cry of pain brought was a laugh from someone, a

familiar laugh and as I looked up see who it was, I not only realized who I had run into, I was also reminded of the answer to my burning question.

Tim! It was my friend Tim I had banged into, or, more accurately, it was Tim's massive shoulder that had brought me to a halt. Tim was also my answer to what I was doing here.

Yes, *Tim* was the reason I was here at the beach today. Tim was the one who had seen the news report on the TV about the giant waves and it was Tim who called me, of all people, to go with him to view this amazing sight. Tim seemed to always be calling me when it came to going places like this or seeing and doing stuff I wasn't sure I could do, or wanted to do. He was always pushing me to do more, more, more; and me, being the dummy I was, usually said, "Yes, yes, yes."

Tim and I were pretty good friends. In some ways he was as close to me as Henry and Richie, and we did a lot together. Tim and I didn't have as much in common as Henry, Richie and I did, but we still spent tons of time planning great stuff.

Where we seemed to be together most often was when it came to water and water sports. That was our common ground. It was also where Tim excelled in life. In fact he was not only good in water; he was *amazing* in it. He was so at home in water, be it in a pool or the ocean or a lake, that he had earned the nickname "Timmer the Swimmer" by us all.

Tim could literally swim faster, dive from higher and stay under the water longer than anyone we had ever met. He had to be part fish! We would sometimes just stand at the edge of the Olympic size pool at the high school near our house; and watch Tim go back and forth, sometimes 3 laps, under the surface of the water and never need to come up for air. People would start to panic and call the lifeguard. "I think he's drowning" someone would shout. "He appears to be swimming down there, but I still think he might be drowning!"

No one believed anyone, especially a kid, could stay under the water that long and not get the bends or something once they resurfaced. I sometimes just left him there to go home because I had to be in before dark. I would reassure kids that it was just "Timmer the Swimmer" doing his thing, and soon everyone knew him as the premiere swimmer in our area. I even thought I saw the lifeguard at the pool marking Tim's distance so he and the other lifeguards could attempt the same underwater distance later.

No lifeguard ever demonstrated their underwater ability during the day for people, especially with Tim around, so I knew their nighttime attempts were in vain.

Tim was also a good friend to have around in times of trouble because of his size. All that swimming had made Tim not only strong, but big as well. His arms were huge and his shoulders were so wide that you never wanted to ride next to him in a small car or, God forbid, a rollercoaster or something like that. I made that mistake only once at the Fair that came to our local Catholic Church once a year. I can only remember the first sharp left turn which sent his massive right shoulder plowing into the side of my left temple, and for the rest of the ride, and most of the night's activities, things were a blur.

"Sorry, dude!" He would say. "My bad!"

"Your *bad* alright."

He was too *big and bad* for his own good. He probably could have pounded the snot out of someone if he wanted to, though I never saw him actually get mad enough at someone to use his size to his advantage. That was also what made him a good friend. I never told anyone this, but I would use his intimidating size, and our friendship, to my advantage whenever possible.

"You better not mess with me" I'd say to someone wanting to mess with me. "My good friend 'Timmer the Swimmer' is going to be here any minute!"

That usually sent the assailant fleeing and shouting something like, "My bad, Johnny! I didn't mean to mess with you! There's no need to bring Tim's shoulders in to this!"

It was those shoulders that had stopped me in my tracks that day at the beach as I attempted to gain a better vantage point for my next Pulitzer Prize winning photo.

Tim also stopped me in my tracks with the next words out of his mouth; words that would change my life forever. I can't believe he said them. I can't believed I heard them and, most of all, I can't believe I responded to what he said the way that I did.

JOHNNY'S SURF FACT NO. 2
Surfboards & surfing products have gone from a fun hobby to a $7 Billion industry annually. Surf's Up!!

CHAPTER TWO:
"THE TIM FACTOR"

Tim had an incredible ability to talk me into attempting anything, and he had been doing it for most of my life. I could still vaguely remember when Tim and I had first met. Our families had moved into the same housing tract and onto the same street only a week a part from each other. Tim and I were both two years old at the time and my first encounter with Tim was in the nursery play area of the bowling alley in town where our parents began bowling together each week. It was there where Tim and I would punch each other, throw things at each other's heads and, you know, really become good friends. At this young age I was still about the same size as Tim and could hold my own. Water and swimming hadn't entered the picture outside of an occasional Slip-n-Slide™ session or a "run though the sprinklers" episode.

As we grew older, however, it became apparent to me, and everyone, that Tim was more than just good in water. He owned it.

The first time he entered a swimming competition at the local pool he won all six events he entered. He also recorded the fastest time ever clocked in four events at that meet for ten year old boys ... and Tim was only eight!

I raced against Tim in only one race that day. A race I had won the year before (Tim wasn't there). But on this day, Tim beat me and all of us by almost a complete length of the pool. I stopped swimming competitively and picked up a basketball instead. I had only taken up swimming because I lived at the beach, but my heart wasn't really in competing, so letting go of it wasn't hard at all. Some kids, who realized they had met their match in Tim dropped swimming as well. Swimming took more dedication than most of us wanted to invest, especially if we knew we were fighting for second place with Tim around.

Tim, however, loved it and the competition, and invested every moment he could in swimming; and it was paying off for him big time!

At ten, eleven and twelve years old, Tim and I would sign up for Junior Lifeguards together each summer. It was a great way to spend part of our summer down at the beach and learn water safety along with becoming more confident when swimming in the ocean. It was also fun!

Tim made captain of his squad each year and at twelve he not only looked as big as some of the real lifeguards, it was rumored that he could swim as well and even out swim some of them.

On the last day of Junior Lifeguards every summer there was always the ultimate challenge of swimming around the pier.

Taking on the waves, the current, and the tide to swim almost a half of a mile and not drown in the process was not something I looked forward to, but Tim loved it!

I can remember standing at the water's edge, looking left and right at all the other junior guards, hoping to spot anyone as scared as I was. I looked for knees that were shaking, and not because of the coldness of the morning beach air, but instead, out of sheer fear. I didn't see anyone looking overly nervous, so if they were they could hide it much better than I could.

I did, however, notice that the number of kids who came on the last day was always less than on any other day. Many had obviously stayed home to avoid this final day and the death-defying challenge that came with it.

I knew that the lifeguards would never put us in a situation that we couldn't handle. I mean, I think they wouldn't. I'm pretty sure they wouldn't. Okay, I didn't know for sure and many kids were so unsure that they came up with whatever excuse they could to tell their parents they couldn't go, or didn't need to go, that day.

They, better than I, had somehow convinced their parents that they were either sick, or maybe didn't need to attend the last day because they had passed all the real important tasks needed to be a Junior Lifeguard that summer. Excuses like the ones I had worked on, in front of the mirror, earlier that morning; but failed miserably at when the time came to try them on mom and dad.

Unfortunately for me, my mom and dad were the type of parents who got overly involved with anything I was involved with, so they knew what was happening even more than I did sometimes. My mom was always signing up to be the "Team Mom" for baseball or "Den Mother" for scouts, and dad was always around to be an assistant coach for any sport I was involved with, sometimes without even being asked. And yes, they even made time to come on the last day of Junior Lifeguards to cheer me on as I attempted the great pier swim. My dad would find a way to go into work late so he could see me surface from the water at the end of the swim. This gave him ample information to share proudly with everyone at his work. That put even more pressure on me to finish the swim and not drown in the process. What would he tell his co-workers?

"Johnny came close this year, but swallowed a little too much ocean, oh well."

Of course I'm joking; they would be heartbroken if anything was to happen to me ... wouldn't they?

They also knew what I was capable of, so they were cautious but confident. Obviously more confident than I was because my knees were knocking so loud that had kids were looking around to see where the noise was coming from.

Tim, spotting my fear, would always start out by me and ease my tension by looking me in the eye and saying, "Follow me, Johnny. Do what I do and you'll be fine."

Great advise except for one thing; no one could do what Tim could do in water! No one my age could swim like him. No one could keep up with him. His words of confidence were not reassuring at all. They just reminded me of how in over my head I was. I just hoped I wasn't in over my head for more than a minute because that was only as long as I could hold my breath under water!

I began to daydream of the horrors that might await me out in this relentless, rough ocean. Maybe I'd get off track and just keep swimming out to sea never to be seen again. Maybe a giant whale, though they were never seen in our region, would come up and swallow me whole. I thought about swimming next to a chunky kid hoping a whale would choose him over me as a meal. Wow, out of self-preservation, I was resorting to unkind thoughts. I was starting to lose it big time.

When I emerged from my daydream I found myself staring at a chunky kid with an evil look on my face. He was looking back at me with a scared look as if he knew what I was thinking.

"I should go over and apologize." I thought.

But there would be no apologizing because my thoughts were interrupted by the loud squeal of an air horn.

The swim was underway and the sand rumbled with the pounding of hundreds of feet racing for the water's edge. A sea of red swimsuits and excited faces began splashing into the water.

"Follow me, Johnny!" Tim shouted as he raced away from me.

I ran after him as fast as I could!

"Don't lose him!" I screamed at myself as I ran for my life in his direction.

But it was no use. Tim hit the water at full speed, dove under the first wave, went into fish mode, and disappeared. He resurfaced twenty feet further out into the water and began to stroke like, well, like only Timmer the Swimmer could.

Basically, he was gone and I was left to swim with the others around me.

I dove under waves and swam against the incoming current. I instantly thought about how much easier it would be to swim when I was on the other side of the pier and traveling with the current as it pushed me towards the shore, but I had an entire pier to get around and bigger waves ahead of me before that would even be a reality.

As I swam I tried to stay in the pack as best I could. No whale was going to single me out. I also tried to relax as I swam so I wouldn't run out of breath or energy too soon. This was a long swim and the goal for me was not to finish first, but to finish alive. My ego would like to see me finish at the front of the pack, but I knew my limits in water, and just a finish would be a victory for me. I did tend to pick up the pace whenever I saw a girl starting to pass me up. Some of them I could stay ahead of, some went by me like I had an anchor tied to my leg.

"They'll tire out." I told myself.

I figured it would be like the tortoise and the hare. They would jump out to an early lead and then I would come on at the end and pass them all up because, well, they were girls. Girls can't out swim guys, right?

Wrong. I never saw most of them again. They left me like I was standing still. So much for my - girls can't out swim boys - theory.

As I approached the end of the pier, far out in the ocean, I thought to myself, "Yes! The half way point! I can do this!"

At that very moment I felt a cramp grab my leg like someone was squeezing my calf with a monkey wrench. I had to stop swimming and stretch my leg before the muscle knotted so much that I couldn't finish. I fought the pain and pointed my toes upward stretching my calf until the cramp slowly went away.

I looked over at the pier to see where I was. I still had a ways to go to reach the end of the pier and I considered, for a moment, cutting through the pier and shortening the trip.

"Maybe no one would notice." I thought to myself. Just then a girl, maybe eight or nine years old passed by me.

"Do you need some help?" she asked as she swam by.

Me, need help from a little girl? Not on her life.

"No, I'm fine." I forced out. "I just wanted you to feel like you were doing better than you are!"

What a nasty thing to say to someone who was just looking out for me. My calf quickly tightened in pain again.

"Okay, God!" I grimaced. "I'll find her and apologize when the swim is over."

As I began to swim again I realized my break had helped my breathing get under control and my stroking improved. I made it around the end of the pier and I felt a surge of confidence knowing I was passed the halfway point. It was also a comfort knowing that I was now swimming with the current. I looked up at the shore ahead and saw some kids already finishing and running up on the beach and passed the flag wedged in the sand about fifty feet up on shore. That was a discouraging sight. How could I, having lived, swam, and surfed in this ocean all my life, not be a faster swimmer than I was? This was also my third year as a Junior Lifeguard and it didn't look like I was any faster of a swimmer than in years gone by.

I started to feel sorry for myself, but my pity party ended quickly as a lifeguard on a paddle board went by and shouted encouraging news.

"You guys will finish in the front half of the group if you swim hard!" he shouted.

That was all I needed to hear. I had never finished in the

front half of the group and though the people on shore were claiming victory, it would be a major victory for me to finish strong. Maybe even Tim would be impressed if I finished in the top half of the group. He was probably on shore, completely dry by now, looking for me to emerge from the sea at any moment.

I raced with renewed strength and began to pass people as I split the water like a dolphin preparing to launch himself skyward and ring the bell at the end of a pole, like I saw them do many times at Sea WorldTM.

I made a dolphin sound, leaped up out the water for a second and took off swimming.

As I neared where the waves were forming I knew I'd have an edge now because I was a good body surfer, and if I could catch one of the bigger waves it could take me all the way, or close, to shore quickly; and with little effort on my part.

At that point, I was willing to let the waves do as much of the work as they would like.

I caught a giant wave and rode it with supreme accuracy. Tim had shown me years ago how to catch the shoulder of a wave and stay out in front of it allowing it to push you along as far as it could carry you. I covered about one hundred feet in a matter of seconds passing swimmer after swimmer. As I neared the shallow water, I heard a familiar "Wahoo!" coming from the shore. It was Tim. He had seen me catch that wave and ride it with precision towards the beach.

When I came up from that wave my feet could touch the ground. There are many great feelings in life, but not too many are greater than touching the sand with your feet once you've been out in the deep ocean as long as we had. I ran, knees high, towards the shore trying to keep my balance. I dove forward a couple of times in smaller waves to get a bit more of a push to the shore. I finally came up out of the water and though I was exhausted and out of breath, I somehow was able to race up past the flag and finish the event. Tim was right there with a high five.

"Dude, you smoked that last part, and shredded that big wave!" He said with excitement.

"Thanks!" I said, breathing hard and trying to remember my name.

"How did you do?" I asked as I panted, knowing he had probably done well.

"I finished first." He said with far less excitement than was due for such an incredible feat.

That was another of the amazing things about Tim. He always let his actions speak louder than his words. It was a great quality that I wished I had but never did.

Tim even beat one of the lead lifeguards that were supposed to swim ahead of the pack as guides! I could see kids looking over at Tim and talking about it. I looked up at Tim to see his reaction.

"I felt good today," was all he could say and I shoved him in disbelief. He didn't budge of course. He was solid, even at twelve.

Tim's solidness was what woke me from that flashback of our Junior Lifeguard days and brought me right back to the incredible event that was taking place with the giant waves in front of me.

I laughed to myself thinking what it might have been like if these were the waves on the day of the pier swim. "Yeah right!" I thought. "Event cancelled for sure!" Well, *maybe* cancelled . . . the lifeguards could be brutal. "No one would be crazy enough to go out in these waves!" I thought, and then Tim shattered my thoughts by finishing what he started to say before I blacked out in my daydream. I didn't like the look on his face.

"Do you know what we need to do, Johnny?" Tim asked as he stared at the mammoth waves in front of us.

"Take another picture?" I said sheepishly, hoping that might be what he was thinking.

I knew he had something a bit more daring on his mind, but I didn't know how daring. I was hoping the "Take another picture" line would let him know I didn't want to have anything to do with anything too crazy.

Of course, those clever lines of mine never fazed Tim when he had something life-changing for us to attempt. Tim had always challenged me to do more. He had been pushing me and pushing me all my life, and I, stupidly at times, would somehow agree to go along with crazier and crazier adventures. Call it ego or just plain ignorance, but something always made me join him.

What he had in mind for me to join him in today, however, was by far the crazy to end all crazies!

"We need to body surf one of these waves!" Tim said with ease and confidence, like he already knew it was possible.

My response at hearing his ridiculous and life ending statement was swift and well thought out.

"Are you kidding me?!" I screamed at the top of my lungs like a little girl who just had her favorite doll snatched from her.

"Come on, Johnny." Tim said. "We can do this! I've got it all planned out!"

"Planned out?" I shouted in fear and anger. "You have my death planned out? You have my last day on this earth planned out? You know that's premeditated murder, right?"

I went berserk! This time Tim had gone too far! Pushing me to be a stronger and more confident person was one thing. Leading me to an ocean grave was another.

"No!" I shouted, and loud enough for him and others around us to hear. "The answer is no, and this time, Tim, no means no! It can't be done"

"It can be done, Johnny!" Tim fired back as if my rant meant nothing to him.

"And just think how it will change our lives if, I mean, when we do it!"

There he went playing the "Change our lives" card.

"Change our lives? Don't you mean end our lives?" I shouted.

"I won't let that happen!" Tim said emphatically. "I know we can do it, unless, of course, you're chicken."

Whoa, the "Change our lives" card followed by the "Chicken" card! That wasn't fair at all. No guy could take that double whammy without a fight! Change my life or not, I couldn't let anyone call me chicken like that, not even Tim. Even if I was!

"I'm not chicken!" I shouted out loud!

"I'm just dumb!" I thought to myself!

"Good!" Tim shouted.

He turned and ran to his bike and returned with two sets of swim fins. I had been so excited and preoccupied at seeing these incredible waves that I had never noticed he had the fins on the handlebars of his bike the whole time. Tim had planned what he wanted *us* to attempt ever since he saw the waves on the news earlier. He didn't bring us here just to see the waves; he brought us here to experience the waves. His confidence in himself was well deserved. His continued confidence in me was astonishing and I was amazed. I also knew that this time I was really in over my head!

I should have just ran and never looked back. I should have taken off while I had the chance. No one would ever look down on me for not being a part of Tim's crazy scheme.

No one, that is, but me, and that thought kept my feet planted right where they were. I was about to enter Looneyville, U.S.A. and Tim was the Mayor!

JOHNNY'S SURF FACT NO. 3
The U.S. Lifesaving Association began beach rescues as swimming gained popularity in the 1800's.

CHAPTER THREE:
"A SUMMER TO REMEMBER"

Saying yes, or more accurately, not saying no to Tim's challenge of even attempting to body surf a wave of the magnitude of these bad boys we were standing in front of brought back the memory of the last time I took on a wave too much for me to handle.

That instance almost cost me my life, and did cause some major bodily ouch-age. I knew I was in over my head then too.

It happened two summers ago when our family, and Summer's family, the Breeze's next door, decided to take a vacation together. We were heading down south to camp on a famous beach known for incredible surfing. I had seen pictures of the waves in a surfing magazine and I couldn't wait to take them on and show them who was boss. I also thought it might be a great chance to show Summer how good I was at shredding waves. Why I wanted to show off at times, and especially in front of Summer, I didn't really know. I did know it usually didn't work out well and made me look even more foolish, but I would do whatever stunt I had planned anyway.

Like the time I told Summer to watch me do a double back flip on the trampoline in her backyard. Had I ever done a back flip on a trampoline? No. Had I ever even attempted a double back flip on a trampoline? No. Did that stop me from wanting to impress her? No.

I can remember her saying, "Don't try it if you don't know what you're doing. You can really get hurt Johnny."

But I was in major show off mode, so all I heard was, "Blah, blah, blah, blah, blah, Johnny."

I had tuned out all negativity, and common sense. I was out to impress her and that's what was running the show in my head.

As I bounced higher and higher on her trampoline I tried to picture an Olympic diver spinning around and around as they leaped from a high platform.

"Just do what they do, Johnny." I told myself. "They're only people."

Yeah, only well trained, extremely athletic, super-human people that spend a lifetime perfecting a dangerous sport so they can represent their entire nation and enter a worldwide event so exclusive that only three people in the entire world walk away with medals.

At the thought of that I should have stopped bouncing, come to my senses, got off the trampoline and gone home. But did I? No, and I still have a small scar on my knee to remind me.

At one point, I thought about making up some kind of excuse to not go through with my attempt to show off, but I looked down and saw Summer staring at me. I also saw Henry and Richie running into her backyard. They had seen me bouncing amazingly high from the street and came running in to see what I was doing. If wanting to impress Summer wasn't enough to make me continue, having my two best friends there pushed me over the edge.

Henry and Richie were the kind of friends that you would think, having heard that their good friend was about to attempt something that might possibly kill him, would step in and tell him to stop, he was crazy! Oh, but not these two. We lived for things like this so we'd have incredible or horrific stories to tell later.

Mostly, we had horrific ones.

That didn't come to mind in time either, so I went for it.

I can remember bouncing one last time, giving it everything I had and throwing my feet up into the air. I curled up into a ball and began to spin backward. The feeling of weightlessness was awesome. I felt like an astronaut must have felt while doing a space walk. I completed the first flip easily and tried to keep my momentum going. That's when I lost sight of where I was, and when gravity began to take over.

"Houston, we have a problem!"

"Which way was up?" I thought as I began to panic. "Which way was down? Where was the trampoline? Where was I going? Why are my eyes shut? How will this end? Am I going to die? Am I getting an iPhone™ for Christmas? Does red and blue really make purple? I want my mommy!"

A lot goes through your head, I guess, when you're spinning out of control.

Panicking was the last thing I remembered. I blacked out, and when I came to, the three of them were standing over me, looking down on me like three surgeons staring down at their patient. I felt like I needed a good hospital right then also. My back felt stiff and my knee was killing me.

"He's alive!" Henry shouted.

"Whoa, awesome!" Richie said as he looked at me in disbelief.

The only kind words came from Summer who asked if I was okay.

"I think so. My knee hurts, but I think so. What happened? Did I make it? Did I do a double back flip?"

I was more concerned about my efforts than the fact that my knee was bleeding and I couldn't walk very well. As I crawled up on a lounge chair, they began to tell me what they saw.

"It was awesome, Johnny, just awesome!" Henry shouted with excitement. "It was the most amazing thing I've ever seen! You flipped about three times in the air!"

"I counted four!" Richie said, cutting in. "You were like a buzz saw up there and when you came down and hit the trampoline it shot you skyward, like a human cannon ball being shot out of a cannon at the circus!"

Henry chimed back in, "Yeah, only it shot you to the left and off the trampoline! You hit that palm tree over there in midair and then came crashing down on your back on the grass! It was awesome!"

"Man, Johnny that palm tree saved you." Richie said. "If you would have missed it, you would have gone over the fence and into the Mrs. Jenkins rose bushes and been slashed to pieces!"

I didn't feel like thanking a palm tree at that moment. I *was* kind of glad I did black out though. I'm not sure I would have liked to have been awake during my death-defying ordeal.

Summer came out of her house with a wet washcloth and

a bandage for my knee.

"Here, Johnny. Clean off your knee and put this on it to stop the bleeding."

"Maybe you'd like Summer Nightingale to clean off your boo-boo for you, Johnny." Henry said sarcastically.

Richie laughed.

They had both figured out by now that I was trying to impress Summer with my back flip into oblivion, and they both snickered as I snatched the cloth from Summer's hand.

But even that trampoline stunt was nothing compared to what I attempted while Summer's family and ours vacationed together. That stunt wasn't adventurous; it was, looking back on it, downright dumb.

When we arrived at our camp space, my dad announced that we needed to put the tents up before we did anything else. My dad wanted the tents up before dark. There was nothing more aggravating, and humorous to me, than watching my dad attempt to put a tent up in the dark; poles flying everywhere, dad tripping over ropes, canvas collapsing, stakes missing. It was quite a show.

"I'll be right back to help, dad!" I shouted. I wasn't going to do anything until I had seen the amazing waves here in person. It was all I could think about on the drive down.

"Come on, Summer!" I shouted as I grabbed her hand and ran for the shoreline.

When we arrived at the water's edge we stood in awe at what we saw. We marveled as big, beautiful waves curled towards the shore, one after another, in perfect harmony. This was a surfer's paradise with clear bluish-green water, white sand, and warm sunshine. It was awesome!

There were some local surfers in the water catching every wave they could and riding them for as long as possible. Some of them could really shred and were pulling off one great move after another.

To our left were two giant rocks about ten feet apart sticking up out of the water and when a wave would crash against them the whitewater would fly into the sky.

"That is so cool!" Summer said, as another wave pounded into the rocks.

There were only three surfers to the left of those big rocks which didn't leave them much water or wave to surf. Waves would start and slam into the rocks in just a few seconds after forming.

"What are those guys doing over there?" Summer asked, seeing them at the same time I did.

"I don't know? Maybe they're just talking or done surfing for the day and just hanging out."

Just then another wave began to form and, to Summer's and my amazement, one of the three surfers began to turn around and paddle as if to catch the wave. When he jumped up on his board and began to surf, I thought to myself, "This dude is crazy!"

He then cut to his left and disappeared behind the first rock.

"Ahhh!" Summer shouted, and for good reason.

From where we stood, it looked like that dude had surfed right into the back of the rock, but then, to our surprise, as the wave was about to crash against the first massive rock, the surfer came out from behind it and shot himself, and his board, between the two rocks staying on his board as the wave crashed into the boulders on both sides of him. He split the rocks and made it through clean.

A few "Woo-hoos" were shouted from onlookers down the beach.

"That was amazing!" I said out loud.

"That was scary!" said Summer.

"That was awesome!" I blurted.

"That was impressive." Summer said with a smile I didn't like.

"That's got to be tried!" I announced, not believing what I had just said.

"That's ridiculous!" Summer said looking at me, not believing what I just said.

"That's happening tomorrow." I stated, trying to sound more confident.

"That will give your sister more room to stretch out on the car ride back home." Summer said smugly as she turned and walked back towards our camp.

"That's not funny!" I thought as I ran back with her.

It was that smile on Summer's face that made me continue to think about the possibility of "Shooting the Rocks" the next morning. I thought about how I would do it. I tried picturing the maneuver over and over in my mind. I burnt two hot dogs in our campfire that night daydreaming.

"Do you want a little mustard on your piece of charcoal there, son?" My dad said laughingly, awakening me from my daydream.

Everyone laughed.

"Hilarious as always dad," I said sarcastically, only

making everyone laugh more . . . at me.

Summer, however, wasn't laughing. She knew what was distracting me and she couldn't believe I was still contemplating the idea.

"Did you ever stop and think why there were just three surfers over there on that side of the rock, Johnny?" Summer asked rhetorically. "They know what they're doing! They probably live here and have spent years surfing these waves. They are probably the only three that feel they have what it takes to pull a stunt like that off."

"I have what it takes!" I blurted out childishly. "I'll show you tomorrow!"

"Don't do this to impress me, Johnny. Trying to kill yourself will not impress me. There are no palm trees out there to save you this time"

"Ouch!" She slammed the trampoline incident right in my face! I grabbed my knee instinctively.

Summer got up and walked over and climbed into her tent. I sat there wondering if I was really going to go through with my threat tomorrow or not. I also wrestled with if I was doing it for me or to impress Summer? I needed Henry or Richie's advise on this one, but they were miles away. Then again, they probably would have told me to go for it so they could record the outcome, good or bad.

The next morning I was up and in my wetsuit early. I grabbed a banana and my board and headed for the beach. When I got there, there were about ten surfers already in the water ahead of me and five or six stretching and getting ready to hit the water. There were no surfers on the left side of the rocks in the "Danger Zone," as I now called it.

There was one guy though, down the beach to my left, stretching and staring out at the rocks. He watched as wave after wave crashed against them almost seeming to be psyching himself up. I got up and ran his way. If he was going out on the left side, I had to talk with him first.

But, before I could reach him he grabbed his board and ran into the water throwing himself over the first small wave. He landed on his board and began paddling out to sea.

I began to slow down, thinking I had missed an opportunity to hear from a master. Then, I felt my legs begin to speed up and the next thing I knew I was racing into the water with my board and paddling like crazy after him. I dove under waves and paddled repeatedly until I began to get close to the place where the waves were forming. As impressive as the waves pounding against the rocks looked from shore, they looked and sounded even more impressive when they were only a few feet away, and I could almost hear those rocks calling me …calling me to my doom.

"What am I doing here? Go back to shore!" My mind kept repeating over and over in my head; but instead, I kept paddling.

When I finally reached that other surfer I could see he was about twenty years old. He looked like he had been surfing for longer than I had been alive. This guy was a pro. He belonged here and maybe I didn't.

As he sat up on his board I saw him look back at me paddling towards him.

"Hey kid, what are you doing out here?" He said with surfer attitude.

"Just checking out the waves," I said, trying to sound

cool!

"Yeah, well, this is where you'll check out for good if you don't know what you're doing!"

"I know what I'm doing!"

"You ever "split rocks" before, little dude?"

"Not here!" I said, which was the truth - in a way.

"Anywhere?" he fired back.

"Sure, dude!" That wasn't true at all.

"Well, this swell is funky. You have to start low, then go high and then finish low or else."

"Or else what," I asked?

He pulled his right leg up out of the water and showed it to me. It had a nasty scar that started at his ankle and then disappear up under his wetsuit.

"Or else this bro; it goes all the way up passed my knee. Eight hours of surgery, dude, and I'm one of lucky ones."

I knew at that moment I should have turned and paddled to shore. Nothing was worth this. Even having Summer smile at me the way she smiled at that other guy yesterday wasn't worth this.

"Turn and paddle to shore!" I told myself.

I would have too had not a big wave entered the scene.

Instead of paddling away, I watched as this guy dropped his leg and moved over into position. He barely had to paddle to catch the wave because of the power it possessed.

He instantly caught the wave, jumped up on his board, gave a quick, "Wahoo!" and took off.

He started low on the wave, too low from what I knew about surfing. The wave looked like it was going to land on top of him, but just then he turned and shot up high on the top of the wave. Too high I thought this time. He needed to move down a bit, but he didn't. He just stayed there, suspended in flight for a second or two.

"He's going to get pitched over the top of the wave and thrown into that rock below!" I thought.

But that didn't happen. Amazingly, he was able to stay high on the wave until the last possible second which carried him just passed the edge of the first rock and then he quickly drove his board downward, just in time to miss the second rock and, somehow, go right through the middle of them. It was by far the most amazing surfing move I had ever seen.

I could hear people cheering from the shore, and as I looked in I could see Summer and her brother, and her mom and dad, and my mom and dad, and my sister all on the shore waving at me. Summer had probably told them what I was up to when she saw that I wasn't at camp this morning.

I knew the right thing to do was to return to shore, but once again, my ego had taken over. I tried to ignore their shouting for me to come in and pretended it was them cheering me on instead.

I paddled my board into position, turned away from them and stared at the waves.

Seeing one I liked, I got into position and paddled. The wave was strong and picked me up instantly moving me quickly towards shore.

"Low, then high, then low!" I kept repeating over and over again in my head. "Low, then high, then low!"

I jumped to my feet and rode to the bottom of the wave moving to my left and closer to monster rock number one.

Again, I heard it calling for me and not in that "Let's go grab a burger for lunch, we're pals!" type voice, but more of an "I'm going to eat you for lunch, pal!" type voice. That unnerved me for a second, but I quickly locked back in to what I was doing.

I stayed at the bottom of the wave as long as I could and then, just before it swallowed me whole, I broke for the top of the wave. I could hear the wave pounding the water behind me as fast as it was forming in front of me. I stayed at the top of this wave longer than a surfer would want to.

Every surfer knows that if you stay too high on a wave for too long it will throw you off like a person being tossed over a water fall, only to have you crash in the churning waters below.

I had stayed high on waves too long before, a bunch of times, but that was by accident. It was never on purpose like this; but what else could I do?

I had to stay high at this point because there was nowhere else to go! Just below me was that first massive rock trying to pull me in and munch me. The sound of the water being sucked towards it almost sounding like it was swallowing everything in sight and I was its next little morsel.

I held on at the top of the wave, not wanting to be just another appetizer to this hungry mass of stone.

I fought with all my might to stay where I was until I could hold on no longer.

I could literally feel the wave trying to spit me onto one of the rocks below, so I had to make an attempt to avoid them and possibly find a way to get between them.

I was just beginning to panic, okay, *panic even more than*

I already was, when I saw what I was hoping for. There it was; the small opening between the two boulders. That slim sliver of hope I knew was there.

"Hey, I just might live to tell this story!" I thought.

Instinctively, I shot down off the top of the wave, doing all I could to try and hit that improbable opening.

I fought the momentum of the wave that was trying to grab me and throw me down onto rock one, or hurl me over onto rock two.

I did all I could to turn my board towards the daylight between the two rocks and thought, for a quick second, I was going to make it too, when all of a sudden the wave gave one violent push to keep me from going the direction I was trying to go.

"It's trying to kill me!" I thought.

I was now dropping and dropping too fast, too soon. I could almost hear the first rock laugh as it began to pull me in.

I wasn't going to make it! It was a scary feeling I would never forget.

I saw myself about to slam into the far edge of the rock, just short of the opening, so I quickly kicked up my board putting it between me and rock and braced myself for the impact. I closed my eyes awaiting my fate.

"Crack!"

My board slammed hard into the rock and it instantly snapped in two pieces and went flying. I went flying too, in the other direction and fell headfirst into the ocean below as the wave pounded the rocks on either side of me.

My arm struck the rock hard on the way down and then

went numb as I tumbled into the water.

As I came to the surface, I was disoriented for a couple of seconds before I realized where I was. I looked up in time to see my dad swimming towards me and the surfer I'd met earlier paddling towards me as well. He pulled me up on his board as my dad arrived.

"Are you all right, Johnny?" My dad shouted.

"Yeah, I'm good!"

"Yeah, you're good for now!" he said with that "punishment awaits" voice I knew all too well.

"I warned him, pops!" The surfer dude said, almost as if he was trying not to get punished too.

"Dude, you're not helping!" I thought to myself.

As we all worked our way towards shore, I looked up at the surfer as I hung on to his board. He put his finger and his thumb close together and whispered, "This close, bro!"

I forced out a quick smile and head nod without my dad seeing.

Then he pointed to the scrape on my arm and whispered, "Battle scars, bro. Battle scars. You'll be back!"

I half-smiled and said, "I don't know, dude. I don't know."

You would think that incident would make me never ever consider attempting anything again that involved big waves and unsafe conditions. But, here I was, standing next to Tim, staring at the biggest waves I had ever seen in my life, and as he handed me a set of fins, I actually found myself sitting down in the sand and putting them on.

Tim gave me a final look of total confidence, and for one

brief moment the fear of the waves went away and, instead, a wave of courage swept over me. Yikes!

JOHNNY'S SURF FACT NO. 4
In the 1950's surfboards averaged
10ft. in height and weighed 50lbs.
Today 5' 6" & 15lbs. is the average.

CHAPTER FOUR:
"WHIRL POOL"

"The only thing to fear is fear itself!"

I don't remember what famous person said that, but I do know who lived by it, and tried to get other fools like me to live by it as well, Tim.

What was it about being around Tim that built up my confidence so much? What kind of evil magic did he have that made me buy into all his attempts to challenge/injure me? Was I so in need of impressing him, or was I just trying to impress myself?

Either way, Tim had caused me to try more things than I ever would have tried on my own, and it did give me a better sense of confidence about myself in the process. I'll thank him when I'm older; if he doesn't get me killed attempting one of his crazy ideas before I *get* older.

As I slipped the fins on, I stared out at the churning water. The ocean was being tossed in all directions by the power of each huge wave as they crashed over and over on the beach.

"If one of these waves was to get a hold of me," I thought, "It would take me down to the bottom of the ocean and try to keep me there!"

Tim might be able to hold his breath under water forever, but I had normal lungs that would only hold air for a normal amount of time, and this situation was *not* normal!

The stirring water reminded me of the last time I thought I was going to drown, and Tim was the cause then too. Was this his mission? Was he a spy for a secret government trying to wipe out guys like me?

"You're mission, Timmer the Swimmer, if you choose to accept it, is to remove Johnny Lazarus from society and make it look like an accident."

The incident I'm talking about happened a couple of years ago. My dad had come home and announced he was going to put a pool in our backyard. My sister and I couldn't believe it. This was awesome news! I ran to tell Henry and Richie the good news!

"Dude, no way!" Henry shouted. "This is awesome! It will give me a place to perfect my cannon ball dives! I'm going to soak the girls at the city pool big time this year!"

Henry's cannon balls were legendary. When his short, chubby body curled up he became almost perfectly round, and when he hit the water the splashes would be huge. No girl was safe anywhere near the edge of the pool. Whether they were talking or just working on their tans, they were targets for Henry and he was deadly accurate. He could soak a girl twenty feet from the edge with a perfect shot. Henry wasn't too popular with the girls at the city pool, and you'd see some of them move away from the edge when he showed up, but the guys loved him and would pick out girls for him to try and bombard with water.

Some of the older guys used Henry's bombs as a way to meet girls by offering them a dry towel, and a little fake sympathy, as they stood there, completely soaked by the cannon ball master.

"How high will your diving board be, Johnny?" Henry

asked. "Ten feet? Twenty feet high?"

"Relax, Henry." I said. "We don't have the kind of money to put in an Olympic Diving Center. Besides, our yard isn't that big. I'm not sure it's even big enough for a built in pool and they cost major bucks."

Richie, like usual, was far more level-headed when I told him.

"That's awesome, Johnny!" Richie shouted. "Anything will be totally great, and close by, and free! We won't have to pay to get into the city pool anymore."

"Except when I'm ready to demonstrate my 'Cannonball Perfectico!'" Henry said with an evil laugh.

"My cousin's dad put an above ground pool in their backyard." Richie said. "It's twenty feet across, four feet high on the edges and almost six feet deep in the middle. It's a blast, and plenty big."

"What about a diving board?" Henry asked.

"There's no diving board, but they built a deck with a platform to jump in the pool from, and yes, Henry, you can do a killer cannonball from it."

"Nice!" Henry muttered. "Let's go, Johnny! Let's go ask your dad what kind of pool you're getting!"

Henry grabbed Richie and I and made us run to my house. I was excited to know too and couldn't believe that I hadn't asked what kind of pool it was going to be before I ran to Henry and Richie. I guess I just hoped my dad had struck oil or won the lottery and it would be a built in pool, with a rock formation, a couple of waterfalls and palm trees like I had seen at the hotels in town.

"Reality check, Johnny." I told myself.

Once again, Richie was the more knowledgeable one. He had thought our situation through and yes, we were getting an above ground pool with a deck and only slightly smaller than his cousins. Ours would be eighteen feet across, four feet high on the sides and about five feet deep in the middle. That was good enough for me.

Construction began that Saturday. I wanted to tell Tim across the street so badly that we were getting a pool. Timmer the Swimmer would probably be as excited as I was that there was water nearby, but I couldn't tell him right then because he was gone at a swimming competition, go figure, and wouldn't be home for another couple of days.

The pool went up quickly and by the following Tuesday we were already filling it with water.

My dad and I were putting a final coat of clear varnish on the wood decking and I looked at the pool in amazement.

"Is this really happening?" I asked myself. It was just too awesome to imagine, and yet, there it was right in front of me. My dad had a look of satisfaction on his face as well.

"Way to go, dad!" I said to him as we painted on the last bit of varnish.

He smiled back at me. Nothing more needed to be said.

It wouldn't be long now, and we'd be the hit of the neighborhood, or at least the hit of our street.

It was going to take a few more hours for the pool to fill up with water, and we needed that time to let the varnish dry on the deck anyway, so I knew to be patient.

"A watched pool never fills." My dad said.

I could hang in there time-wise, but Henry couldn't. Being patient was not a phrase in Henry's vocabulary.

He would stop by every hour, on the hour, to look in and see where the water level was. Filling of the pool was going slow. The hose had been in the water for a couple of hours but the water level looked like it was only about a foot high.

"Uhhh!" Henry exclaimed in disgust. "Are you sure there's not a hole in the bottom somewhere Mr. Lazarus?"

"No hole, Henry. It just takes a lot of water to fill a pool this size. You could grab a paint brush and help us finish putting on this last coat of varnish."

"Uh, no, um I have to get home for lunch or I would."

"Yeah, right!" I thought as I laughed. Henry ran from work like a dog that had just snatched a hot dog off the plate of an unsuspecting kid at a backyard birthday party. Come to think of it, Henry had done that too.

That night, the pool was finally filled. My dad had installed lights so that the pool would glow a bright turquoise blue in the dark.

"Can we go in, dad?" My sister and I asked repeatedly.

"No, let's let everything set and let the varnish on the deck dry over night. You can go in after school tomorrow."

After school? How could I wait until after school to go in? Shouldn't getting a new swimming pool be some kind of holiday?

The next day, as I got ready for school I was so excited about the pool that I actually thought about wearing my swim trunks under my pants.

I wasn't crazy enough to do it though. The rubbing might leave a nasty rash. I needed to get a grip on myself. I took one last look at the backyard to make sure the pool was really there and assure myself that all this wasn't just a dream.

There it was, shiny and blue and refreshing looking. I couldn't wait to get back home.

School could be slow at times. There were days where I just stared at the clock knowing that someone in the office was holding the hands in one place just to torment all of us students. But none of those days matched the slowness of this day.

Between classes I ran into Henry and Richie in the hall. Henry came running up excited, as usual.

"Is it ready? Is the pool ready, Johnny?"

"Yep, today is the day. That is, if school would ever end."

"I know what you mean." Richie said. "It's like the clocks have stopped."

"Maybe they need new batteries?" Henry blurted out.

"Well, for one Henry, they run on electricity not batteries, and two, the electricity is fine or there wouldn't be lights on in the hall here." Richie said in his usual, well thought out way.

"Well, it had better end soon!" Henry said with a sense of urgency. "I've got my swim trunks on under my pants and they're starting to rub."

I take back what I said about swim trunks under your pants being too crazy for anyone to do. There was one person crazy enough to do it.

As the bell rang we all headed for our next class. Only two classes to go and then splash down! As I walked to class I saw Tim. He had come back from his swim meet last night. Up until now, I hadn't seen him or had time to tell him about our pool.

"Tim!" I shouted as I ran to catch up with him. "We have a pool; a swimming pool in our backyard!"

"A what? No way!"

"Yes way! It's an above ground pool and its' awesome. We're going in for the first time after school today. Come over when you get home. I know it's not some Olympic size pool that you're used to, but it's still a pool."

"Totally, and there are a lot of fun things you can do in those kind of pools." Tim stated as he headed for class. "I'll be there for sure, dude!"

"Cool! Hey, how did you do at your swim meet?"

"I won all my events!"

Of course he did. He was Timmer the Swimmer.

School finally ended and I raced home fast, almost like I had been let out for the summer. I ran up to my room and threw on my trunks.

"I'm heading out to the pool, mom!"

"Okay. Henry's already out there, but I told him he couldn't go in until you got there."

Richie was just walking in the backyard when I came out from the house. We high-fived and then headed for the pool. Henry was up on the platform and appeared to be doing some kind of measurement study in his head. He was looking around and pointing and pondering. I could tell what he was thinking.

"Hey Henry!" I shouted. "It took an entire day to fill up this pool. Let's not empty it with just one of your world-class cannonballs!"

"Don't worry guys. I'll start small and work my way up. Besides, I can do cannonballs that send the water straight up and straight down. They're big, but you don't lose any water."

For some reason we both believed him. His accuracy was legendary.

Just then, Henry, having finished his calculations, leaped into the air, curled up into a ball and headed straight down towards the middle of the pool.

"Cannonball number one!" He shouted, just before he hit the water.

Henry was right. His cannonball created a huge splash. Maybe ten to fifteen feet in the air, but the water went straight up and came straight back down into the pool. Barely any water went over the edge at all. It was amazing to watch a master at work.

"Nice one Henry!" Richie shouted as soon as Henry broke the surface of the water.

"It was okay, but it needs work." Henry said.

Henry dove while Richie and I swam. We splashed, and we laughed for at least an hour. We played a few rounds of Marco Polo and then we all just relaxed and floated on rafts for awhile.

A voice broke the silence, "Ready for some real fun, dudes?"

It was Tim. He had come over to check out the pool. I jumped off my raft and pushed Henry and Richie off theirs.

"All right! Timmer the Swimmer is here. Let the games begin!" Henry shouted.

Tim laughed and climbed the deck to the platform. He did a perfect jack knife dive and went into the water without a splash. It was the complete opposite result of a Henry dive but equally as impressive. How Tim could dive head first into an above ground pool and not smack the bottom was a mystery to all of us. We knew better than to try it and my dad had already laid down the rule on no head first diving, but Tim seemed to be the exception to the rule.

Tim proceeded to stay under the water and go back and forth across the pool six times without surfacing for air. It was an amazing sight and we gasped each time he reached the edge and, instead of coming up, turned and pushed off again for another lap. Then he stopped in the middle of the pool and just laid there on the bottom for awhile.

"How long do you think he's been down there?" Henry asked.

"I don't know, but it's longer than all three of us could stay under combined." I said.

"Oh yeah! Watch this!" said Henry.

He then took a big breath and dove down under the water. Henry shamefully resurfaced before Tim did.

"Okay, he's good." Henry sputtered as he gasped for air.

Tim finally came up and without even sounding winded said, "Nice pool, Johnny. Nice pool."

Then Tim took over as recreation leader of the pool.

"Okay." He said. "Pool Game No. 1, Whirl Pool!"

"Whirl Pool?" I asked myself.

Henry, Richie and I had spent most of the afternoon coming up with game after game. We thought we had figured out, mastered, and played every pool game known to man too. But, in just this first game Tim introduced us to, Whirl Pool, we realized we were mere pool game amateurs.

Whirl Pool seemed like a simple enough concept when

Tim first explained it to us; but we soon found out it was not as easy as it looked. We also learned, after playing it just once, that it was by far the best game we had ever played and it instantly became our favorite pool game, and the first one we would all play whenever we got together from that day on. Way to go Tim!

Whirl Pool went like this. We would space ourselves equal distance from each other around the edge of the pool. So close to the edge that we could touch the wall with our hand. Then, at the command of someone, we would all begin to walk in the same direction around the edge of the pool, circling it. The goal was to see if we could get the water in the pool to join us as we walked and created a whirl pool effect. The faster and harder we pushed the quicker and faster the water would begin to join us, and pretty soon, if we gave it our all, we could actually get the water to spin in a circle around the pool, and spin fast.

Tim would encourage us to drive harder with each step and faster with each lap.

"If anyone gives up now the whirl pool will be lost!" He would shout.

We pushed our legs and bodies through the force of the water until defiantly, inch by inch, it would join us. I would look at Henry, but not when he was looking at me. His face was so funny looking when he was trying to push the water that I would crack up laughing and inadvertently stop pushing.

One time, maybe out of exhaustion, Henry grabbed one of the rafts on the deck as he passed and locked it under his arms as he pushed. It seemed to help him move more water and kept his head above the surface area.

"Great idea!" Tim shouted at Henry. "Everyone grab a raft when you go by the deck! Let's make this one huge!"

We pushed and pushed and soon we had the water spinning violently and swiftly around the pool and that's when the fun began.

Floating in the water and having it do all the work to take you around the pool was awesome. You could just relax and circle the pool for a long time without touching the bottom, or needing to swim at all. The "Whirl Pool" did all the work. We'd play tag and chase each other using big giant steps to do so. Tim tried to circle the entire pool in as few steps as possible using the current to move him along. He looked like a slow motion long jumper in the Olympics. It was hilarious to see and soon we were all trying it.

Richie shouted, "Hey, I'm Superman!" and he proceeded to go under the water and turn his body so his stomach would rub along the side of the pool. He put his arms out in a Superman flying position and sailed along under the water as if suspended in air. He stuck his head up occasionally for a gasp of air and then back he'd go. This had to be tried, and it was a blast.

Whirl Pool became the game of games in the pool, and soon, everyone that came over was introduced to Tim's genius game and we all had an awesome time!

Another great thing we learned was, the more people in the pool running around the edge; the quicker we could get a whirl pool started and the faster and longer it would go.

Friends at school began yelling, "Whirl Pool" at me in the

hallway when they would pass by. Our pool had become a great place to hang out. Tim had really come through. Having a swimming pool in my own backyard was amazing. It was the greatest thing ever to just put on your trunks, go out back and play for hours, and yet, I still recall the day that I almost stopped swimming in the pool and gave up swimming all together for that matter.

It was about a month after the pool had been put in. Henry, Richie and I were relaxing on rafts after a great day of diving, swimming, Whirl Pool and Superman.

Henry was lying on his back and calculating what kind of cannonball it would take to send water over the fence and into Summer's bedroom window on the second floor of their house.

"It can be done!" Henry said, without letting us know what he was thinking.

"Maybe it can be, but it had better *not* be!" A familiar voice announced from outside the pool.

It was Summer. She had come over to just relax in the pool but her sixth sense had picked up on Henry's thinking. She was good at knowing what Henry, Richie, me, or anybody might be thinking before they acted on it. She kept me from doing some pretty dumb stuff because of it too.

"Hi Summer!" I said while trying to spin over on my raft. I fell in the water, of course.

"Hi Johnny!"

"Again with the "Hi" instead of "Hey" when it comes to Johnny," Henry whispered to Richie.

"Let it go, Henry!" Richie whispered back.

We all still somewhat believed in the theory that Richie's older brother had told us about that if a girl was to say "Hi" instead of "Hey" to you, it meant she liked you and maybe even like-liked you.

Henry and Richie were sure that Summer like-liked me and that I must like-like her because we spent so much time together.

As much as I tried to shun the idea, every "Hi Johnny" from her just gave them more ammunition to fire back at me.

"Grab a raft and jump in." I said quickly. I could see the smirks on Henry and Richie's faces.

"All the excitement is pretty much over for the day."

But oh how wrong I was.

"Don't put that raft in the water just yet Summer. It's time for pool game number two."

It was Tim's voice echoing from outside the pool. He was standing at the edge and he flicked water at Henry as he spoke.

"What's up, Dr. Splash? Are you ready for some real high water," Tim asked?

"Bring it on!" Henry exclaimed, not really knowing what he was getting himself into.

None of us knew.

Henry didn't know. Richie didn't know. Summer didn't want to know, and if I had known what the outcome was going to be, I would have *said* no. But I didn't know, so I didn't say no, and so, you know, I did a no-no.

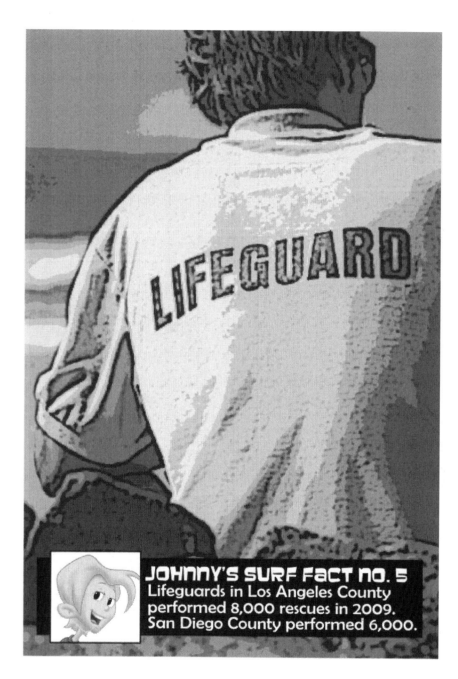

JOHNNY'S SURF FACT NO. 5
Lifeguards in Los Angeles County performed 8,000 rescues in 2009. San Diego County performed 6,000.

CHAPTER FIVE:
"DON'T MISS THE CYLINDER"

Did you ever do something and then think afterwards, "I probably should have thought that through better?" For example: " I probably should have put up a large piece of wood behind the dartboard I hung in my room today."

Why does that come to mind after you've thrown the first dart, missed the dart board completely, and put a giant, *dad's going to freak out*, hole in your bedroom wall?

I never really learned much from these types of incidents, so when Tim suggested I join him for "Pool Game No. 2" I was an easy target. Unlike my dart board.

"'Pool Game No. 2' had to be fun," I thought.

After all, Tim's "Pool Game No. 1," Whirl Pool, was a huge hit!

"Let's hear it!" I said as I stood there in the pool with Henry and Richie.

"Get the rafts out of the pool and I'll show you" He said.

Tim then climbed up the side of the deck, went on the platform and, again, did a perfect jack knife dive into the pool with no splash. It had become his calling card.

"You can join in too, Summer." Tim said.

"No, I'll just stay on the deck here and observe thank you."

Summer had mastered the ancient art of "Think it through!"

"Come on, you don't even know what it is Summer."

Henry exclaimed. "It could be a blast!"

"If it is, I'll jump in."

"Jumping in is the key!" Tim said. "Now everybody come to the middle of the pool."

We all did what he said. He was, of course, Timmer the Swimmer.

"Now, everyone, at the same time, start jumping up and down."

"What," we all said questioning him?

"Just do it and you'll see what happens," he fired back!

And, at Tim's command, we did what he asked. We jumped …and jumped. We felt foolish, but we kept on jumping. We laughed at each other only to have Tim tell us to concentrate and keep going. I saw Summer snickering out of the corner of my eye, and for good reason, I thought.

But then, just before we had reached the point of complete ridiculousness, something amazing began to happen. The water in the pool slowly began to join us and go up with us when we jumped and down with us as we traveled back downward. Pretty soon the water began to almost take over, sending us higher and higher with each jump. It was an awesome feeling. We were soaring five feet off the bottom of the pool, then six, seven and onward to nearly ten feet. We were forming a huge water cylinder in the middle of the pool with each push from the bottom. Water began to splash over the edge of the pool with each thrust downward, but the pool didn't seem to care. This was awesome!

Summer had stepped back, away from the edge of the pool, to the back of the pool deck and she watched in amazement as we dropped below her and then jetted high in the air over her head.

We were all laughing and screaming at the same time! Tim had done it again! "Pool Game No. 2 - *The Cylinder*" had even a better feeling than, dare I say it, *Whirl Pool.* We were defying gravity and it felt awesome!

Tim shouted, "Keep it going! I want to try something!" He then pushed away from the cylinder and worked his way to the edge of the pool and climbed out. The water practically threw him out with one of the downward surges.

"Keep going! Make it big, really big!" Tim shouted as he ran out of sight around the side of my house.

We didn't know what Tim was up to and we didn't really care. We were having too much fun.

A few seconds later, as I soared up and passed by Summer, I could faintly see the look of horror on her face as she stared passed me and towards the roof of my house. I turned while jumping and saw, to my amazement, Tim standing on the edge of my roof. He was facing the pool.

"What was he up to?"

"A couple more big jumps and then everyone get out of the pool!" Tim shouted.

"Why?" Henry sputtered, swallowing a bit of water when he spoke.

"Just do it and you'll see," Tim fired back!

We pushed off a few more times with all the force we could come up with and then dove for edges of the pool. The water spit us out of the pool like a baby spitting out a spoonful of nasty baby food.

For the first time, being out of the pool and out of the cylinder, we were able to see what we had created with our efforts. It was a giant cylinder of water shooting high into the air with every push of water.

"It's twenty feet high, easy!" Henry shouted.

It wasn't twenty feet high, but it was close to ten!

"Here goes!" shouted Tim as he stared at the movement of the water. He began to time the point when the cylinder of water would reach its' peak with every thrust.

He then, to our amazement and horror, leaped from the roof, jumping as high as he could, and threw himself outward towards the center of our pool.

We all gasped, but I could see a smile on his face as he reached the point where the cylinder would eventually rise up to meet him and Tim arrived there just in time to meet the water with pinpoint accuracy, ten feet in the air.

I could now see he was trying, no succeeding, at diving into the cylinder right when it reached its' peak. Tim had successfully turned my five foot deep pool into a ten foot deep pool.

"He's nuts!" Richie shouted.

"No, he's Timmer the Swimmer!"

The dive only lasted a few seconds, but it seemed like everything was happening in slow motion. Tim entered the cylinder head first in a perfect dive and he shot down in the suspended tube of water. For a second, as he traveled downward, I thought I saw him glance over at me and wink as he passed by.

Then, just before he hit the bottom, and before the cylinder could crash down on top of him, he arched his body, bending his back with incredible flexibility. He turned himself ninety degrees from the direction he had been traveling, skimmed the bottom of the pool and shot over to safety at the pool's edge.

When he popped up out of the water, he jumped up onto the deck, threw his hands in the air and gave out a huge shout.

"Yes! Cliff diving at Acapulco!" He shouted.

We didn't know exactly what he meant, but the whole thing was a sight to see; an awesome sight to see!

"That was awesome Tim!" I shouted. Everyone agreed.

Everyone except Summer. While she wasn't being a downer about it, she just wasn't being overly excited either. She did seem to have an impressed look on her face though. A look that would be my doom because when Tim asked who was going to be next to try this daring feat of watery death, I was looking at her face and I spoke up.

"I'll do it!" I blurted out to the amazement of Henry and Richie, and myself.

My "Think it through" skills were under developed for sure.

I stopped looking at Summer, I didn't want to see the look on her face. She would be impressed, once I made the dive, and that's all that mattered.

"Are you sure about this?" Richie asked.

"No." I said to myself.

"Yes!" I said out loud, trying to sound more confident than I was.

I jumped in the pool and motioned for the others to join me. We all began to jump once again, this time with less humor on our faces and more a look of determination. We bounced and bounced creating another great cylinder of water. It maybe wasn't as high as Tim's, due to the loss of water from the first try, but still, it was big. But was it big enough?

When it reached what Tim determined was its' maximum height, he motioned for me to get out of the pool and begin my ascent to the roof of my house. I pushed under the water on the next drop and swam to the edge. I, like Tim before me, was practically spit out onto the ground. I got up and raced to the fence on the side of my house.

I took one look back at the cylinder and thought, "That's not so bad looking. This will be easy, and impressive, and will score major cool points at school tomorrow once the rumors begin to circulate."

Oh, and Summer will probably be impressed too.

When I reached the fence next to my house I was dripping wet and shivering. I hoped I was shivering because I was cold and not just crazy nervous. I was also barefoot and stepped on a rock while running. It hurt badly, and I wanted to stop, but I knew those guys were giving their all in the pool and I had to go through with this.

I climbed the fence and worked my way up onto the roof of my house, skinning my knee on the rough, sandpaper-like shingles in the process. Not even that was fazing me now. I was focused on the task at hand and so I kept moving. I walked softly up the roof to the top because I didn't want my footsteps to let my mom or sister know I was on the roof. I wasn't sure if I would get in trouble for being on the roof. I had never really done it without permission; but this was no time to find out.

I had to reach the top of the roof and then go down the

other side to get to the backyard area near the pool. As I reached the top I could hear the noise of the water pounding and splashing. I could also see the guys coming up with the water and then disappear again and again and again. It was an amazing thing to see. I crept down the roof slowly until I was near the edge and one thing hit me right away that almost made me go back and forget the whole thing. The height of the jump, and the distance I would have to leap out looked ten times higher and further from up here than it did when I was on the ground. It all looked doable from down there, but for some reason, everything seemed bigger and scarier from up on the roof. I began to shiver again, but not from the cold. This time it was because I was starting to become, no, I was, scared to death.

I crept down a couple more feet towards the edge of the roof. I must have looked like a kid who heard noises in his closet and was carefully going to check it for the Boogey Man.

Tim caught a glance of me and waved me on. I walked inch by inch towards the edge feeling less certain with each step. Tim motioned to Henry and Richie and the three of them dove under the water and headed for the edge of the pool leaving me to face this water monster alone. Each time the cylinder came up to its' peak I imagined it reaching out and swallowing me whole.

"Had it become alive?" I thought to myself frantically. My mind would always play tricks on me in moments like this. My dad said it was because I had a good imagination. Well, I kind of hoped I was imagining all of this and if I rubbed my eyes a couple times it would all be gone. Then I heard a strange knocking sound. I looked around and saw nothing. I looked down and saw that it was my knees knocking together. Okay, this was serious scared.

"Now, Johnny, now!" Tim shouted. Tim, Henry and Richie had moved to the deck and were waving and cheering me on. I was talking to myself so much I could barely hear what they were saying, but I knew they were shouting anything they thought would give me the confidence to try this crazy dive.

I then caught a glimpse of Summer. She wasn't cheering. She was just holding on to the edge of the platform. She almost looked like she was praying for me. I hoped she was. I was going to need all the help I could get.

"Well, I've come this far." I said to myself. "There's no turning back now!" Actually there was, but I was again out to impress the guys and Summer and once I'm in "impress-mode" I'll do almost anything.

I took a couple more little steps to reach the edge of the roof and positioned myself right in front of the cylinder. I would need to jump up two or three feet and out about seven or eight to reach the point where the water was at its' highest. I wasn't sure I could leap that far. I knew I couldn't with my knees clanging together, so I reached down and grabbed them to hold them still for a second. Doubt and fear were racing through my mind.

"What to do? What to do?"

"Do it now!" Tim's shouted, with the voice he would use over and over in my life. A certain voice that challenged me time and time again, and could make me try things I'd have never tried on my own. I sometimes hated that voice because

I usually gave into it and attempted some major scary things. I'd most likely thank him later in life for building my confidence, but I didn't feel like thanking him right now however. I felt like strangling him for talking me into this.

"Go now, Johnny and time it right because you don't want to miss the cylinder!" Tim shouted. "You don't want to miss the cylinder!"

Ahhh! I hadn't thought of that! All my thoughts were on timing the jump to reach the water at its peak. I hadn't really thought about what might happen if I missed the cylinder completely. When the water went down towards the bottom of the pool the center of the cylinder would almost disappear leaving only about a foot of water. Landing in that wouldn't be good. I couldn't let that happen!

Jumping fifteen feet into a foot of water was going to leave a mark for sure!

Then I saw Richie about to speak.

"Talk me out of this Richie!" I thought to myself. "Talk me out of this, old friend, old pal Richie!"

Surely he had my well-being in mind. He must have calculated the situation and found there to be too much risk involved.

"Save me Richie with your words of wisdom!"

"Um, Johnny, you need to go now because the cylinder is starting to get smaller! I've calculated a loss of about three to four inches in height each time it thrusts upward, so go now!"

"Thanks, pal!" I said sarcastically inside my head.

Richie was right though. The water was losing momentum. It was now or never!

"Now! Never! Now! Never! Ughh . . . Now!"

I watched the cylinder two more times intently and started counting in my head. "One thousand one, one thousand two, and, when I saw the cylinder rising on three, I leaped high and out as far as I could from the roof so that I would have a chance at hitting the water at its peak. My timing was perfect, or so I thought.

As I reached the point where I knew the water would reach me I turned and began a hands first dive downward.

There it was. The water was coming up to greet me. It was an awesome sight looking down into the cylinder's center. It seemed to be inviting me in so I reached out my hands, threw my feet high in the air, and straightened my body like an Olympic diver would before entry into the pool. I waited for my hands to hit the water and then have the cylinder swallow me whole.

"Nice!" I thought to myself. "I'm going to make it! I'm going to live!"

But, like usual, just when I thought everything was in place. Just when I thought I'd hit the water … the water stopped, looked at me, laughed, and then turned and left, leaving me suspended, hopelessly, about ten feet in the air.

"I missed the cylinder!" I shouted in a panic.

"He missed the cylinder!" Henry and everyone on the deck shouted.

All my calculating and planning had been off by just a split second and instead of the water ride of the century, I was about to freefall into the shallow water of doom below.

"Maybe I could just stay up here until the water came back up again? Maybe I have the hang time of Michael

Jordan? Maybe I can defy gravity...Nope."

Down I went, like a huge boulder being dropped down a
well. A well with no water in it! I saw the bottom of the pool
coming at me fast so I curled up in a ball and covered my
head awaiting the impact.

When I hit the shallow water, I hit with such force that it
didn't do anything to help break my fall. I slammed against
the bottom of the pool knocking the wind out of myself
instantly.

As the cylinder regained its momentum and headed
upward again it swallowed me whole and began to toss me
around, under the surface like a rag doll. I began to panic and
felt the need for air so I quickly opened my mouth and
breathed in forgetting where I was. Instead of taking in the
air I so desperately needed, I took in a large mouthful of
water which caused me to start to gag. Still feeling the need
for air I breathed in, if you can believe it, through my nose
this time.

"Yee-ow!" Water up the nose stings like crazy!

It also doesn't help when you're out of breath,
underwater, hurt, and don't know where you are or *who* you
are, for that matter.

I don't really remember all that happened next. All I kind
of remember was being pulled by some strange force to the
top of the pool and when I broke the surface I began choking
and spitting out water violently.

"Get air!" was all I was thinking. "Get me some air!
Dirty, smoggy, aerosol filled! I don't care what condition it's
in, I just need it and I need it bad!"

When I finally gained my senses and began to actually

breathe a bit, I realized that I was draped over the edge of the pool. I was being held up by Tim and he had my arms and head hanging out of the pool.

Tim had dove in the pool, grabbed me around the waste and pulled me to safety.

I turned to look at him, not knowing if I wanted to thank him for saving me or strangle him for getting me into this mess.

He looked at me, and when he knew I was going to be okay he simply said, "Now wasn't that great?"

"No, that wasn't great!" I shouted as best I could while still trying to get my breathing under control.

Tim had almost done me in, again, and instead of apologizing, he was trying to make this into a great adventure that only he could give me. That was it. I was going to let him have it this time, verbally. I certainly couldn't harm him physically. He was huge!

"No, that wasn't great!" I started in again and I was really going to tell him what I thought until he leaned over and whispered something only I could hear.

"Remember, Summer's here." He said quietly.

Oh man, he had stopped my verbal attack in its tracks. He knew how hard I would go out of my way to impress her, and Henry and Richie for that matter. I could turn this into a whining session, and with good justification, or I could, as Tim pointed out subtly, make this a triumphal moment.

I gave Tim a quick smirk and said again. "No it wasn't great!" Then I continued. "It was *more* than great! It was awesome! The leap from the roof, the sense of weightlessness, the fall, everything! It was totally awesome!"

"What about the landing and almost drowning part!" Henry said with a bit of disgust.

"Okay, I didn't time it right, but that comes with trying huge things like this, right Tim!" I was laying it on thick.

"Right, Johnny!"

"I don't know, Johnny?" Richie said, jumping in the conversation. "You looked pretty darn scared up there on the roof."

"Yeah, your knees were banging out sounds like a conga drum!" Henry said with a laugh.

"That was just the cold air hitting me, but I was preparing my mind the whole time. I knew without a doubt I was going to do this!"

I wondered if they were buying any of this baloney I was serving up.

"What did you think, Summer?" Tim asked looking up at her.

I had forgotten to look up and see her reaction. I could read her face pretty well sometimes.

"What did I think?" she repeated. "I think you're going to be in huge trouble because your pool is half empty, your backyard looks flooded and I can see your dad pulling into your driveway from here."

"Yikes!" I shouted. "Help, I need everyone's help!"

But before I could finish the sentence the guys were gone. Henry and Richie took off around the house and Tim leaped over the fence into Summer's backyard and made his escape. Only Summer was left and she started to walk off to go home.

"I don't suppose you want to help me, do you?" I asked.

"You reap what you sow, Johnny. You reap what you sow!" she said as she walked to the corner of the house. She turned the corner a disappeared, but then her head peaked back and she said, "Nice dive, Johnny."

She smiled and disappeared again.

Was she giving me a compliment or being sarcastic? Had I impressed her or looked like a fool? Maybe I couldn't read her face as well as I thought after all. I'd ask her later if I ever got up the nerve.

I could read one face very well though, my dad's, and I jumped when I saw it staring at me through the window of his bedroom. He was looking at the pool and the backyard and he wasn't pleased.

I ran and grabbed the hose, turned it on full blast, and threw it into the pool; then I grabbed a nearby broom and began sweeping puddles of water onto the grass.

"Dry puddles, dry!" I repeated over and over in my mind as if they would actually hear me and evaporate instantly, saving me from the "Wrath of Don."

A slap on the back!

No, that wasn't my punishment for the pool incident. A week without going in the pool was the punishment for that. Talk about being grounded.

A slap on the back, just now, was what woke me from my backyard haze. It was Tim slapping me on the back and bringing me back to the present and the horror that awaited me in the ocean in front of me. The waves here were making the cylinder at my pool seem like the little "plop" a pebble would make when you dropped it in a pond.

"Time to go, Johnny! Let's do this!"

He pulled me to my feet and pushed me towards the water. I almost fell over, forgetting I was wearing swim fins. "The shoes I'll most likely be buried in. "I thought.

"Where was my dad when I needed him?" I said to myself as panic began to set in. "I could sure use a week's grounding right now!"

But my dad wasn't here to save me. Summer wasn't here to talk me out of this. It was just me, Tim and these monster waves!

I snapped one final picture of Tim with a huge wave crashing into the pier in the background. I figured it would help identify my assailant should I not make it through this. Tim, the pier, the waves; one of them might be the cause of my demise, or maybe all three and I needed to leave proof behind.

I walked over and tucked my camera into one of the towels Tim brought.

Towels . . . I never saw the towels, I never saw the swim fins, I never saw any of this coming.

JOHNNY'S SURF FACT NO. 6
Huntington Beach, CA has such
a great surfing history that it
adopted the name "Surf City USA"

CHAPTER SIX:
"AND PYLONS TO GO BEFORE I WAKE"

As Tim and I walked towards the water I could see the excitement on his face growing. To me it seemed more like a death march.

"Dead Johnny walking!"

One of the scariest parts was how the ground shook beneath us every time a wave slammed against the shore. They were so big and powerful that they would literally rock the earth around us. It was like an ongoing series of earthquakes, or one big one with aftershocks that kept coming and coming.

Unfortunately, there was no place to duck and cover.

I flapped slowly in my flippers until I met Tim at the water's edge. Tim was watching and timing our approach. He wanted us to get a good start in the water, so running in as the water was retreating back into the ocean was critical. We had to be in as deep of water as possible before the next wave hit or we might be planted in the sand permanently.

"Get ready!" Tim shouted.

He needed to shout too because the sound of the waves crashing into the pier and pounding down on the sand was way loud.

"I'm as ready as I'm going to be, Tim!"

"Good! This should be easy. We'll swim out there where the waves are just forming, then we'll swim through the pier to get to the good waves on the south side."

"Wait, wait, wait!" I shouted back. "Did you say swim through the pier? The pier being slammed by waves! The pier in jeopardy of being destroyed by the on slot of waves! The pier that has been closed by the lifeguards due to possible damage! The pier that is barely visible due to all the whitewater engulfing it by these world class waves! Swim through *that* pier? Is that what you said Tim? Tell me I was hearing things. Tell me I misunderstood you due to the boom-boom-boom of the relentless waves pounding the pylons!"

"Don't worry, Johnny. I'll meet you out there and we'll go through together. Have I ever let you down?"

Had he ever let me down?

"Don't miss the cylinder!" came to mind, but it was probably better not to bring up any negativity right now.

"Now, Johnny, now!" Tim yelled as he took off for the water.

I ran as fast as I could after him, fins flipping over and over again.

"Don't fall down, Johnny! Don't lose him!" I kept repeating to myself as we hit the water and began to wade out.

The first few feet were easy because the rush of the water from the previous wave was returning to the sea so swiftly it was actually pulling us out with it. A couple more strides with our legs and then Tim and I leaped and dove into the water at the same time. We swam as fast as we could, using the outgoing current to our advantage. We were both moving along pretty good and I was actually keeping up with him for the most part.

"Heads up!" Tim shouted as he pointed out to sea.

I looked up and saw a massive wave coming our way! I had dove under many waves in my day and knew the feeling of having a big wave pass just over your head as you hugged the bottom trying not to get caught up in its current. The bigger and more powerful the wave, the more it tried to get a hold of you as it passed. It almost felt like a high-powered vacuum trying to suck you up like a stubborn piece of dirt wedged deep in someone's carpet.

I took a breath as the wave crashed in front of us and dove under the wave going as low and close to the bottom as I possibly could. Tim disappeared just ahead of me doing the same maneuver.

The noise of the wave rumbling towards me was louder than I had ever heard from a wave before and as it began to pass over me, I knew this whole idea of swimming out to sea wasn't going to be easy, or fun. I hugged the ground and even though I was grasping for sand at the bottom and kicking my legs as hard as I could, the wave still got its hooks in me and pulled me backwards violently. That's when I really knew I was in trouble. As I came up for air I couldn't see Tim for a moment and I began to panic.

"Keep going Johnny" I heard from about thirty feet ahead of me and over to my right. Tim had made it a bit further than I had, but we both still had a long way to go.

"Go at an angle, not straight ahead when you go under!"

I wasn't sure what he meant by, "Go at angle." at first, but then I saw him dive under the next wave at a forty-five degree angle to his right instead of straight ahead. Tim was telling me, and showing me, that using an angle approach to the left or right might work better in dodging the pull of the wave versus taking it head on. It was worth a try.

I swam hard to get as much of the ground back that I had lost in the last wave and prepared myself for the next one.

"Are we having fun yet?" I thought to myself.

As the next wave pounded ahead of me I watched Tim dive under slightly left this time and so I tried diving at a slightly right angle. The wave jerked me, violently, but I again pumped my legs as hard as I could and did everything possible to stay low. It still pulled me back some, but for some reason, it didn't catch my legs as much as before and I was able to surface quicker and recover a bit faster. I had no idea how Tim knew this angle diving would work to fight the current the way it did, and I didn't want to know. I just wanted to stay alive and keep moving.

Tim was even more in front of me now, a hundred feet or so. I decided I'd try to make up some of that ground on the next wave. I swam hard and tried a big leap to the left this time. Unfortunately, I timed this jump wrong by making my dive too big. I didn't make it all the way to the bottom before the wave arrived and angle or not it caught me and sent me flying backward. When I came up I had lost a lot of ground and now I was also scary close to pier.

"Okay, no more super dives!" I said to myself. "Just angle and go, angle and go!"

By this time, Tim was out of sight and that made me nervous, and yet, more determined at the same time. I dove and swam for what seemed like an hour or more. The huge waves were beating me up pretty good. They were also making me tired. I was now at a point where I could no longer touch the bottom, so I was relying on my arms, legs and fins to keep me going. I was losing energy fast, breathing hard, had swallowed about a gallon of saltwater, and I was still only at the halfway point. I thought about turning around and heading back a bunch of times, but as I looked back towards the shore and saw how far I had come, I pressed on.

When I finally reached the spot where the waves were no longer crashing down, just forming, I was amazed how high the waves would take me in the air as I sailed over the crest of each one. It felt like I was going as high as the pier some times. When I sailed over the top of a particularly big wave I saw two distinct things.

One, was Tim who had been out here waiting for me. I don't know how long he had been out here floating around, but he did look well rested, so I knew he had been here awhile.

"All right, Johnny!" He shouted when he saw my little head peak over the wave at him.

The second thing I noticed, when I looked over at the pier, was the crowd of people leaning against the rail and staring at us intently. Even though the pier had been closed, the word must have gotten out that there were two crazy kids that had decided to take a little swim in these storm-like conditions. That had to be seen, and whether they broke through the barriers or knew someone that let them through, they were here and wanted to know why we were.

I heard a man yell down to us, "Go back to shore! It's not safe!"

I glanced up and could see it was a lifeguard.

"What do we do now, Tim?" I shouted. "We're busted!"

"He's going to have to come out here and make me leave!" Tim shouted back. "Besides, were not breaking the law!"

Maybe we weren't breaking any laws, but we were certainly putting ourselves at risk and it was the lifeguard's job to prevent that from happening. In his eyes we were doing something wrong; seriously wrong!

"What to do?"

"Follow me!" Tim called out, as if he was answering the question in my head. I swam over to him and I felt a sense of relief just being close to him in the churning water.

"After the next big wave, we swim through the pier as fast as we can!"

"Are you sure we can make it?"

"If we swim hard and don't get distracted, we should be good." Tim said. "Oh, and don't crash into a pylon!"

"Should be good? Crashing pylons?" Tim was *not* helping my confidence.

I thought about calling up to the lifeguard for help but Tim interrupted my thought with a loud shout.

"Now!" And with that he took off, swimming faster than I had ever seen him swim before and that was fast! I had watched him glide through pools and lakes with the speed of dolphins before but this time he looked like a dolphin on steroids!

I took off after him.

"Come back here!" I shouted under my breath, and I swam with all of might. Tim was already well ahead of me and pulling away. I swam even harder and watched for the other side of the pier. I also watched the pylons and made sure I swam far enough away from them so that the current wouldn't pull me into one of them. They were covered in sharp mussel shells right at sea level and hitting one of them or even rubbing against one would probably cut me up pretty good.

As I reached the halfway point I heard the sound I did not want to hear, at least not yet.

"Boom!"

I knew what it was, and I looked down the middle of the pier towards the sea and there it was. A huge wave was coming through the pier and was starting to slam against one pylon after another as it worked its' way closer to me. I swam even faster. Fear was putting my stroking and kicking into overdrive.

"Boom!"

That one sounded even louder and it shook the pylons around me.

"Keep moving!" I said to myself. "Don't look up to see where it is. Just know it's close and getting closer!"

That's all I needed to know because any delays now would have it reach me too soon.

I heard one last giant "Boom" as I reached the last pylon. I also felt the water around me starting to rise. The wave had reached me. I kept swimming hoping that it hadn't reached me too soon. I was no more than two or three feet clear of the pier when the peak of the wave washed by sending me fifteen feet closer to shore. I swept passed a pylon and missed it by only a foot or so. I could almost feel its disappointment at not being able to take a shot at me.

"Denied!" I shouted at the pylon as if it were alive.

"Over here, Johnny!" Tim called out. He had been there surveying the area while I was trying not to kill myself. Tim had found what he thought was the perfect spot to take off on one of these waves-to-end-all-waves. "This spot is perfect!" He said. "It's far enough away from the pier and close enough to catch the wave at its highest point! Just be sure you go right and stay swimming to the right once your ride is over."

The current was pulling hard towards the pier on this south side, so if you stopped swimming away from it, it might suck you back into it before you could react.

"Okay, Johnny! This is why we came here! Let's make history! We take the next wave to the beach!"

I grimaced.

We both looked out sea and saw a wave beginning to form; a big one. Tim gave me a look like he had just opened a Christmas present and got exactly what he had been asking for all year. I probably looked like I got nothing but coal in my stocking.

Just then the wave arrived and Tim and I turned to body surf it. When it reached its peak, I looked down at where the bottom of the wave was and it was *waaaay* down there. It was at least fifteen or twenty feet down; maybe even further!

I gasped with fear and pulled back trying to escape the gravitational pull of the enormous wave around me. It was trying to pull me down and take me under. It wanted to send me to the bottom and wipe the ocean floor with my limp body. It was pure evil. I could feel it literally trying to take me in its grasp.

Remember when I told you my dad said I had a huge

imagination? Well, I was not imagining this (very much that is).

Anyway, I was in trouble, and so, with one final jerk I pulled myself free from its grip and miraculously escaped its clutches.

Tim, on the other hand, was totally committed to riding this bad boy, and with a loud, "Ya-Hoo!" he was off.

As Tim took off, the wave threw him out of the water and when he came down he landed on the face of the wave and to my surprise, instead of being swallowed up by the wave, Tim began to slide down the waves face, almost like he was a human water-ski.

He stayed on the surface of the wave and once I could see he had himself under control, Tim began to turn himself to the right using the power of the wave to direct him.

As he moved away from me, I continued to hear him shout with joy as he skidded along the water all the way to the bottom of the wave. He was actually able to maneuver himself wherever he wanted to go. The momentum of the wave was pushing him at a fast speed and shooting him like a torpedo shot from a battleship.

Then, almost as fast as his ride began, it ended. I saw the wave curl above him and then come crashing down on top of him.

"No!" I shouted as the violent crash of the wave sent a thunderous "Ka-Boom!" for miles down the beach.

"Tim! Tim!" I screamed!

I stared at where he had gone under. Fifteen seconds went by and then twenty; thirty seconds, and then what seemed like a minute went by and nothing; no Tim.

I feared the worst and instinctively began to swim his direction to try and find him.

"Please be okay."I said to myself as I began to swim in a panic.

I had seen Tim stay under the water for long periods of time before, but was this too long?

The answer to my question, and major relief, came when I saw an amazing sight up ahead of me.

About two hundred feet closer to shore, an arm with a hand clinched in a fist came bursting up out of the water. Tim's body followed as he shot up in the air with a loud cry.

"Yeeeeessss!" he screamed at the top of his lungs!

"He's Alive!" I screamed inside my head.

He had made it! I was so relieved, at first. Then panic returned as I realized I was going to have to finish the task at hand! I was going to have to attempt the same death-defying feat.

Suddenly, I was awakened from my pity party by a loud noise, but it wasn't the sound of waves crashing. It was coming from the pier, not the ocean, and as I turned and looked up I realized the noise I was hearing was a roar of approval from a crowd of people on the pier. They had gathered on the rail of the pier and watched Tim's amazing body surfing demonstration. They got to see what they had come to see. Someone take on one of these waves and conquer it! Tim was there hero . . . and now I, of course, wanted some of that action!

"Go for it, Johnny!" Tim shouted as he dove under the next wave that passed us. He was in the danger zone, so I knew I'd better take the next wave so he wouldn't keep getting hit.

I turned, just in time to see the next wave coming. It looked, to me, like the biggest wave of the day.

"Oh great!" I thought. "This was it!"

If I was going to leave this planet, I figured I might as well go out in style. I paddled myself over to the perfect position and watched as the wave moved in on me. I could hear my heart pumping with excitement and fear. There was no turning back now.

"What was I doing here?"

Before I could answer my question, however, the wave was upon me. I turned and instinctively began to swim but didn't really need to. The momentum of this wave was so great that it took over and began to move me along with it. When the wave reached its peak I looked down to its' bottom and it looked like at least a twenty-foot drop. This baby was bigger and higher than even Tim's wave!

I thought hard, again, about trying to break free and save myself the horror that awaited me, but this wave was having nothing to do with letting me go. It had me in its clutches and the grip was tight.

The next few seconds would decide if listening to Tim had been a good thing or a bad thing that day.

"Can I have a do-over?"

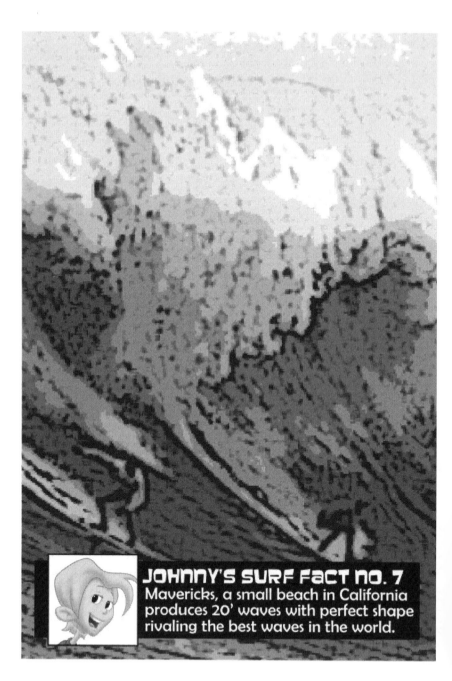

JOHNNY'S SURF FACT NO. 7
Mavericks, a small beach in California produces 20' waves with perfect shape rivaling the best waves in the world.

CHaPTeR seven:
"A WAVE OF COURAGE"

I felt like an article of clothing being thrown into a washing machine. The dirty clothes were tossed in the barrel, water would rush in and eventually the machine would start to agitate and stir everything inside. The clothes may try to put up a fight, but the machine would be too powerful and determined, and so, it would toss the clothes around and around causing the clothes to give in and go with the flow. It must be devastating for the garments. No wonder socks occasionally disappeared, or better yet, escaped.

But for me, there was no escaping! This giant wave was beginning to agitate and stir, and fighting it was useless.

The wave grew and grew and as I reached its' peak, the point of no return, I braced myself for whatever was about to happen. Looking down to the bottom of the wave I realized that if I didn't slide down this wave like Tim did his, the drop would be painful for sure. A twenty foot drop into the mouth of this wave would not be pretty.

I braced myself, waiting to see what this wave had decided to do with me. It held me high in air for just a moment, almost like it too was deciding what to do with me. Would it keep me moving forward or cast me aside like a Del Taco burrito wrapper once the burrito was gone.

Fortunately, it had decided not to squeeze me into a ball and throw me away, but instead, play with me a bit longer.

Much like Tim's wave, it through me up in the air and out

in front of its face. I fell from the sky and landed on the front of the wave near the top and began to slide on my chest downward. I was moving at an incredible speed. I was going so fast that I was outside of the wave and skiing down its front side. I was kicking my legs out of instinct, but it did no good because my fins were actually out of the water. I could hear and sense the top of the wave chasing me. The roar of the water seemed to sound more like an evil laugh and so I turned my head and shoulders to the right and my body followed. I shot away from the pier and sailed right, running from the crashing wave behind me. Being able to maneuver myself as well as I could somehow made this freakishly scary event seem kind of fun. I began to test my ability to go wherever I wanted on the wave and it worked. I could go down and up, a little left and a little right. This was awesome. I began to get even more confident.

"I own this wave!" I thought as I shot right and picked up speed.

"Wahoo!" I shouted out loud! I was having a blast!

"I hope this wave never ends! I'll ride it into the next city. I'll just keep going south until I reach Mexico. Viva el Monster-o Wave-o!"

I failed Spanish. Can you tell?

Of all the great moments in my life, instead of the ride of doom I thought it might be, this one was beginning to creep up the chart and become a great one if not the greatest one ever. The exhilaration, the freedom, the speed, everything! I was riding the wave of a lifetime and was going to live to tell about it. I had conquered my fears. I was attempting the impossible and pulling it off. I was going to escape tragedy,

92

defy the odds and live to body surf another day!

However, as you might have guessed, this wave had a different idea.

Why was it, whenever I had a chance to turn a bad idea into an awesome adventure God always seemed to have other plans?

"Come on God, can't I learn a lesson by making this a dream come true instead of a nightmare?"

"Come on, wave, don't you want everyone I share this story with to think the best of you? Don't you want to be known as Mr. Nice Wave? ...I guess not!"

The saying, "So close, and yet so far" applied perfectly here. I was just a smidge, an itsy-bitsy smidge away from escaping disaster but would miss it by a mile."

"Come on wave! Give a guy a break, and not an *'ouch'* kind of break, a 'Get out of Jail Free Card' kind of break!"

But this wave had other ideas and, once again, just like miscalculating my rotations on a trampoline, just like being inches away from *splitting rocks* while surfing on vacation, and just like being only a split second away from reaching out and making it into the cylinder at the pool, I was close, so close I could almost taste it.

The wave, however, had already made up its mind not to let me taste the thrill of victory; not on his watch. He had decided to see how much I liked the taste of saltwater instead - by force-feeding it to me.

The moment of truth came right at the point where everything seemed to be going smoothly; right at the point of feeling safe. Isn't that always the way things go?

In the midst of my bliss something amazing and weird

happened. Everything around me seemed to turn green. The water in front of me, my skin, my trunks, my fins, everything! It was like I was in a green bubble or something.

"Whoa, Martian City!" I thought.

I turned to look behind me and saw what was causing this "Verde-Grande," (again, F- in Spanish) and to my horror, I saw the culprit. Looking back, or more accurately, looking up, I saw for the first time the wave I had been riding and it reached high into the sky. So high it was, literally, blocking out the sun and everything else for that matter.

It was huge and scary and awesome! It stuck up in the sky like a giant green wall of death ready to take out anything in its path.

Unfortunately, *I* was the only thing in its path, and the wave knew it, I knew it, Tim knew it, and everyone on the pier knew it!

Again, the sound of the rushing water seemed to turn to an evil laugh, and when I looked directly at it, the wave appeared to have a face on it; a sinister looking face with glaring green eyes and an evil grin with gnarly green teeth.

It looked down on me as if to say, "You're mine!"

I was now more scared than I had ever been in my life and as the wave hovered over me I knew it wouldn't be long before it would come crashing down on top of me. I looked around for a way to make my escape but there wasn't one.

The laughter from the wave grew even louder and at one point I thought for sure I heard the wave say, "Lunch!" and I didn't bring one! Ahhh!

I took what I knew was most likely my last breath ever and waited for the inevitable.

It was kind of like being sent to your room by your mom for doing something wrong and waiting there, forever, for your dad to come home, walk in the house, hear the situation, and come in and deliver the punishment.

It was usually swift and just, but never a good thing. I can even remember sitting on the end of my bed one time and dreading the "Wrath of Don" so much that I began to hope and pray that, for some reason, my dad would forget where we lived.

Maybe he'd be on his way home, turn a corner and say, "Hey, where am I?"

Maybe he'd have a momentary lapse in judgment and instead of driving home, think he was supposed to meet some friends in New York and drive across the country. Surely mom would have forgiven me by the time dad worked his way back home. Yeah, that could happen!

I tended to create any scenario and believe anything during the dreaded "Wait for dad."

That was how I felt at this moment, but seeing the wave about to hit me with all of its fury made me wish it was my dad doling out the punishment instead.

I closed my eyes, held my breath, stiffened my body and "Boom!" the wave hit me with everything it had. It grabbed me and threw me deep into the ocean, twisting and turning me in all directions.

I felt like it was trying to rip me apart piece by piece. I bounced off the bottom of the ocean floor a couple of times and was spun around again and again. I didn't know where I was or what to do. Tim had been held down, under the water on his wave for at least a minute. Tim could hold his breath that long but I knew I couldn't and I began to panic. Panicking wasn't helping. I knew that. I knew it would probably cause me to run out of air sooner, but I was beyond scared and panic had taken over.

My next thought was to try and fight the force of the wave and take over the direction I was traveling, but it seemed to have a strong grip on me and was holding me under. The evil laugh of the wave, though now muffled by the water, continued. I had to find a way to break free and somehow swim to the surface before my lungs burst.

I began to fight the current as best I could and swim towards what I thought was the surface, and reach the air I needed desperately.

I kicked my legs and stroked with every bit of energy I had left.

"I've got to keep going! I've got to keep going!" I repeated over and over again as I fought to gain ground.

To my horror, I was gaining ground, but in the wrong direction. I was so disoriented by the tossing and turning that I had gotten vertigo and instead of reaching the surface with my efforts, I hit the bottom instead.

Not being able to see a thing in the murky water made me unaware that the bottom and not the surface was fast approaching and so, it caught me off guard and my head slammed into the sand.

I didn't have time to decide if I was injured or not from the blow. I was on the bottom, the farthest distance from the surface and was running out of air fast. I turned and pushed off the bottom with everything I had and began to swim straight up. I knew I was now, most likely, going in the right the direction but could I hold my breath long enough to reach the surface? I didn't know how deep in the ocean I was and that wasn't helping my nerves.

My throat began to quiver as I began to near the point where I couldn't hold my breath any longer.

"Where is it? Where's the surface? It's got to be coming up soon! It's got to be!"

Just then, the water above my head began to grow brighter, and just as I was all but out of breath I broke the surface of the water.

I took in a huge breath of air and just in time!

Relief swept over me as my lungs finally received the oxygen they had been crying for.

"I'm saved!" I yelled.

Or was I?

As relief began to set in, and my vision cleared, I looked out and realized I was only a few feet away from one of the pier's mussel shell covered, slice you to ribbons, pylons and the current was pulling me towards it.

"Yikes!"

I had gone out of the frying pan and into the fire!

I needed to move away quickly or I'd be slammed into the shells that wrapped it and be cut severely.

I tried to swim away but I was completely drained of energy and could barely move my arms. My strength was gone so I closed my eyes and braced myself for the impact …but it never came.

At that moment, as the water thrust me forward toward the pylon I felt something or someone grab my right arm and pull me back with even more force than the current itself.

It was Tim. Tim had swum all the way back from where he was, trying to figure where I'd surface, if I surfaced, to try and save me and he guessed right. He pulled with all of his might and rescued me from smacking into the pier.

"Are you all right, Johnny?" He said with genuine concern. He probably thought for a moment or two he had killed me with his little "Let's body surf the biggest waves on the planet" stunt.

"Yeah." I said between breaths. "I'm okay. My head hurts though!"

"Your forehead is scraped up pretty good, but you made it! We made it!" He shouted!

"Barely!" I sputtered while coughing up seawater.

"But wasn't that great," he asked with enthusiasm?

"Great? No, that wasn't great! That was dumb!" I thought to myself.

I couldn't think of anything *great* about almost being swallowed whole by the sea, and he needed to know what I really thought about him putting me in such danger.

We ducked under another wave, allowing the current to pull us closer to shore. As we swam in I was thinking exactly what I'd say to him when we reached the shore.

Ah, shore! I never wanted to be on solid ground more than at that moment and when we finally washed up on the beach I crawled up and hugged the sand. We both stayed down on our hands and knees for a bit, looking down at the sand while trying to catch our breath.

"Hi sand. I love you sand!" I said, hopefully not out loud.

Tim looked over at me, both of us still panting a bit and said with a smile, "Come on, now wasn't that incredible?"

"Okay, that was it, here goes!" I said to myself. "It was time to let the mighty Timmer the Swimmer have it! It's time to put him in his place!"

I would have let him have it too if it wasn't for the noise, the bizarre noise of people clapping and shouting.

Tim and I both looked up at the same time and, to our amazement; saw a crowd of people standing on the shore in front of us. They broke into applause once they knew we were okay and ran down to us to congratulate us for our incredible feat.

"Way to go guys! That was awesome!" Someone shouted.

"You made my day, man!" One guy said.

Wow, we were celebrities! These people had come to marvel at the waves and got an extra bonus as well; two guys attempting the impossible and pulling it off!

"I need a picture of this" a lady said making Tim and I pose for her.

We pulled off our fins and stood up proudly. Everyone broke out their cameras and snapped pictures of us. Even a photographer from the local newspaper took a couple pictures and asked our names. People asked other people to take pictures for them while they stood next to us. Tim and I actually started to feel important. We loved it!

"Are you going back out there and do it again," one man asked with humor in his voice?

"No, that was a once in a lifetime thing!" Tim said, and I was relieved to hear him say it.

"Good answer!" said a stern, deep voice from over to our right. We looked over and saw a jeep on the sand and three lifeguards standing in front of it. They all had their arms crossed and a look of disgust on their faces.

"Uh oh!" I whispered to Tim.

"Can we see you boys over here for a minute?" said the man standing in the middle.

He wasn't asking us as much as *telling* us to come over; so we did.

"Busted." Someone said as we headed their way.

The badge on the main guy's jacket read Lifeguard Captain and we knew, just by looking at him, we were in the presence of someone with serious authority. I began to feel nervous until Tim spoke up.

"Hey, Captain Bowman." Tim said with a calm voice.

He knew the man! He actually knew the Lifeguard Captain! How? I didn't know, but I felt a bit more relieved than I felt busted that he did. Tim must have met him during Junior Lifeguards or at a swim meet or something.

"Hello Tim." Captain Bowman said. The sternness in his voice hadn't changed.

The pleasantries were over. The Captain continued.

"Now, even though you boys haven't really broken any laws, you did put yourself in harm's way enough for me to take some kind of action here. This is my beach and I protect it and all the people who come here like they are family. I protect them with my life, understand?"

"Yes, sir!" We both said.

"What are my options to keep this kind of dumb behavior from happening again, Lieutenant Weisser?" he asked of the guy on his right.

"Banning them from the beach for life comes to mind, sir."

"What? They couldn't do that, could they?" I asked myself.

"Yes, we can do that!" the Captain said as if he had read my thoughts.

"What if we promise not to do it again?" Tim jumped in.

"I don't know, seems too light of a punishment to me. What do you think Weisser?" The Captain barked.

"Maybe that and a week of beach clean-up would be enough. Sound about right, Captain?"

"Good call!" Captain Bowman said with a smirk. "You boys are here every morning *at five a.m.* for the next seven days to do trash duty, got it!"

"Yes, sir!" again was the only thing that came out of our mouths.

"Okay, be sure to check in with Lieutenant Weisser here on the pier at Tower Zero tomorrow, and don't be late. Now get off my beach before one of these hero worshipers of yours decides to try the same stupid stunt!"

"Yes sir!"

We ran for our bikes, grabbing the towel, our shirts and my camera on our way. We raced away laughing quietly until we were far enough away to not be heard; then we broke out laughing hard the rest of the way home.

We talked about how incredible the whole day had been. We swapped stories of each of our rides on our wave. We both tried to say we had the bigger wave but that didn't really matter. They were both mega-huge!

I had decided not to let Tim *have it* after all. He had made me a bit of a celebrity, so I let him off easy this time.

We pedaled onto our street and I went up my driveway

and he went up his.

"Maybe I'll see you tomorrow!" I shouted as I pulled into my garage.

"Okay, maybe we can do something together."

"Let's not go to the beach!" I yelled laughing.

"Good call!" he fired back.

I walked in the kitchen and smelled something cooking in the oven.

"What's for dinner, mom?"

"One of your favorites; fish sticks." She said with a smile.

"Fish sticks? Noooo!" I shouted as I ran up the stairs towards my room. "No dinner for me thanks!"

I was hungry, but I didn't want to eat or even be around anything that came from the ocean for a long time!"

I fell asleep the minute my head hit my pillow. I was exhausted. I slept right through dinner and into the evening.

When I woke I had that disoriented feeling you get when you sleep at a different time of day than you usually do. It read eight o'clock on my clock radio, but I wasn't sure if it was eight in the morning or eight in the evening. I sat up in my bed and could feel the dry sand pouring out of my hair; hair that was now knotted up in a nasty bird's nest.

"Nice doo." I said, looking into the mirror on my bedroom wall. I also saw the scrape on my forehead given to me by the ocean bottom. It was a little souvenir to remind me of my voyage to the bottom of the sea.

It hurt to the touch, so I stopped touching it after three, "Ouch!" no, four times.

I walked over to my window and leaned out to see how

dark it was outside. By the darkness of the sky I now knew it was nighttime.

I looked across at Summer's room and could see she was in there hanging up clothes in her closet.

I called to her, "Summer!" and she looked up and came over to her window.

"Hi Johnny!" she said. "How was your day? Did anything interesting happen?"

I spent the next twenty minutes telling her the entire story. I told her about the size and power of the waves and the challenge from Tim. I described in detail the swim out to the big waves, and most of all, my incredible, one of a kind, body surfing ride to end all rides. I didn't leave out a thing. I was going out of my way to try and impress her and, unlike most people, she just sat there listening to everything I said. She even seemed to be interested and enjoying the story. That was one of the best things about Summer. She was a great listener.

"You probably don't believe me!" I said once I realized I had probably been talking too long.

"I do believe you Johnny; every word."

"You do?"

"Yes. In fact I saw the whole thing!"

"You saw? How? Were you down at the beach today?"

"No, I saw you on the six o'clock news! A camera crew from Channel 11 was there and filmed the whole thing. They showed close ups of you taking off, disappearing and coming up out of the water. They even showed Tim coming back to rescue you from crashing into the pier."

"Me! I was on the news? Why didn't you call me?"

"I yelled your name a bunch of times, but you never woke up! You were out cold! I even tried throwing a CD case in your room to try and wake you. Nothing worked …I need the CD case back by the way."

I looked around and saw the case on the floor.

"Man, the six o'clock news, that's huge! What did they say about me?"

"Well, mostly they talked about how dumb of a stunt it was and that you were lucky to be alive. They also focused on Tim's daring swim back to rescue you. That amazed everyone in their studio. They considered what kind of friend Tim must be to put his life on the line to save yours."

"You know, he really is a good friend, Johnny." Summer said.

"I know." I said, finally taking my mind off myself. "He has always been there for me. He always looks after me. He has also been challenging me to do more and try more things my whole life, and I'm a more confident person because of it. I owe him huge!"

"You guys spend a lot of Saturdays together. Have you ever thought about asking him to spend a Sunday with you?"

"You mean, at church?" I asked.

"I can't think of a better thing to do to show your friendship to someone than to introduce them to the God who made them, gave them their incredible abilities, and loves them unconditionally," she stated with confidence.

Summer was right. I had always gotten together with Tim to plan great adventures here on earth, and yet, I'd never considered helping him plan his eternity. Was I being a truly good friend to Tim or not?

Heaven is, of course, the greatest adventure of all and definitely worth sharing, not only with good friends, but everyone.

JOHNNY'S SURF FACT NO. 8
Jack O'neill invented the wetsuit in 1950 so he could surf the cold ocean waters of San Francisco & Santa Cruz.

CHAPTER EIGHT:
"THE FRIENDSHIP FACTOR"

The next day, I walked across the street to talk with Tim. I had decided to invite him to church on Sunday and see what he said.

Talking about church with friends always made me a bit uncomfortable. In fact, I had never really talked to Henry or Richie about church or invited them to join me on a Sunday for that matter. This got me thinking about what kind of friend I really was. I mean, if I didn't share what was most important to me with my best friends, then what kind of friend was that?

After the events of yesterday, and Tim's heroic act on my behalf, I felt we had passed the so-so friend stage and now anything and everything was open for discussion. He had continually helped me with my confidence and I was calling on it, and God, now to help me say just the right thing to him.

Unfortunately, Tim's mom answered the door and told me that Tim was off on another important swimming competition and he'd be gone all week. As I walked back across the street, I was bummed to know I had missed a great opportunity.

At the halfway point back home, Tim's mom called out, "By the way, thanks, Johnny!"

"Thanks for what?"

"Thanks for being such a great friend to Tim. He told me how you helped him get through a tough situation yesterday and that you were a great friend to have around."

"Uh, okay, no problem." I called out.

"I helped him?" Leave it up to him to spin everything around like that to make me look good.

Summer came out on to her lawn as I walked back towards my house, so I gravitated her way. That always seemed to happen when she was around.

"I just heard something weird." I said.

"That was probably my dad snoring again!" she said.

We both laughed as we sat down on her front yard.

"How does it feel to be a celebrity, Johnny?"

"Yeah right! No one has even called or anything. I think you were the only one that recognized me on the news last night. Are you sure you had the right pier? Are you sure it was Tim and me and not two other guys that tried the same stunt later on?"

"It was you all right. I can spot you anywhere, Johnny."

"Oh really? I don't know whether to be flattered or scared. You're not some kind of stalker are you?" I said teasing her.

"You'll never know." She said with a mysterious look on her face.

Wow, I didn't know if I liked that look or not? Maybe I did. Maybe I didn't. Maybe I should change the subject, and quick!

"Uh, am I a good friend to people Summer?" I asked with a nervous voice.

"I think so." She replied. "Do you think you're a good friend, Johnny?"

"I thought I was, but then I thought about what you said last night about what a good friend would really do and now

I'm not so sure."

I shared with Summer all the planning Tim and I had done over the years. How we would get together a month before school was even out for the summer and we'd plan our beach days. We really only had the ocean in common, but that was enough to do a lot of planning when you lived near the beach. Tim and I would write out a calendar for June, July and August every year. We had every beach day planned. Where we would go and what we would do. Surf on Mondays, body surf on Wednesdays, body board on Fridays and so on. We'd surf the cliffs one day and hang out near the pier the next time we got together. The only thing we would allow to disrupt the schedule was a crucial swim meet for Tim or possibly a family vacation. Some summers I would stay at Tim's house while my family went a vacation to a place I wasn't interested in going to. Who wanted to go to Reno, Nevada in the summertime anyway?

Our summer schedule still gave me plenty of Henry and Richie time. So much so, that they probably didn't know how much time I actually spent with Tim. They filled the Tuesdays, Thursdays and weekends. That was more than enough time to be around Henry. He was a wild man. One day with him was like three or four with anyone else. My time with Tim was sometimes like a Henry detox!

Richie was always more under control and never drained you like Henry would. Richie was the perfect *ying* to Henry's *yang*.

Henry, Richie and I would also do summer planning. We would put together events and plan sports stuff more fit for solid ground; instead of water. Over the line baseball, our crazy basketball shot challenge, skateboarding at the local skate park or high school, and Richie always had a bunch of cool websites or YoutubeTM videos to watch and laugh at. Those were all great times. I guess I was pretty lucky to have such great friends which again led me to wondering if I was returning good friendship for friendship received.

I was kind of starting to miss not seeing Henry and Richie. I couldn't wait to tell them about my beach adventure. It was going to take a couple of days for my pictures of the waves to be developed, so they might not even believe me without proof.

"I like our times together too, Summer." I said. "I like our summer vacations together, even if I know it gives Henry ammunition to tease me. I even like it when we sit here and talk occasionally with no one to interrupt us."

Oh, man. I spoke too soon. I barely got the "no interruption" line out of my mouth when I was cut off by the billowing cry of the wild *Henry-bird*.

"Johnny, my man!" He shouted with excitement, as he and Richie raced down the street on their bikes. "There he is! There's the superstar! Johnny "Superstar" Lazarus!"

He threw his bike down on the sidewalk and ran up, dove on the grass and pretended to kiss my feet.

"I can't believe it. I'm actually in his presence!" Henry continued in the typical over the top, Henry way. Summer was dying laughing at Henry's antics.

"Could you translate this for me Richie?" I asked as I pulled my feet away from Henry's lips.

"We saw you! We saw you and Timmer the Swimmer on

the news last night! We saw everything! We tried calling you but your line was busy!"

"It was awesome!" Henry blurted out. "I've never had anyone I know be on TV before, except for my uncle Steve who held up a sign at a baseball game, but he held it in front of his face so no one knew it was him except the few of us who knew it was his sign. That counts, right?"

"Whatever!" Richie said.

"Oh, and check this out!" Henry reached in his back pocket and pulled out a folded up section of newspaper. He opened it and shoved it in my face.

"You made the newspaper too."

He was right! It was a story about the huge waves and the picture the reporter had taken of Tim and I was placed above the article. The caption read, "Local bodysurfers, Tim Phillips and Johnny Lazarus tackle giant waves and win!"

"Wow, the six o'clock news and the local newspaper. Awesome!" I thought to myself.

"Can I keep this, Henry?" I asked.

"Yeah, I bought ten more papers. I'm going to use these at school to score major points!"

Good call. Being the best friend of a celebrity at our school was almost as good as being the celebrity yourself. When we found out that Benny Cochran's cousin was a background dancer on High School Musical, he was treated like royalty for a good month or more.

"It must have been awesome to body surf those giant waves, Johnny!" Richie said.

"Yeah, it was scary, but worth it!"

"Whoa! Check out that nasty scrape on your head! Battle

scars! Cool! Hey, why didn't you invite us to go? I could have rode one of those bad boys too and got my picture in the paper!"

"Yeah, right, Henry!" Richie scoffed. "You get queasy on a Slip 'n Slide™."

We all laughed together; all of us except Henry.

"Ha, ha, ha!" Henry snapped back.

"Hey, where is Tim anyway!" Henry shouted, trying to change the subject. "He's the big hero!"

"Did he really save your life?" Richie asked.

"Not my life, but he did save me from becoming one with a pylon that had my name on it!"

"Ouch! That would have felt below average!" Henry said with a laugh.

"Yeah, Tim has been taking care of Johnny all his life. Johnny and I were just talking about that, weren't we, Johnny." Summer stated.

"Yeah."

"In fact, Johnny was trying to decide what the best thing was that he could do to show all his friends the true friend he really is, right Johnny?"

"Uh, yeah, I guess so."

"Did you want to share with Henry and Richie what we came up with?" Summer continued.

I knew what Summer was doing. She was trying to get me to finally ask Henry and Richie to come to church with me next Sunday. Summer was always challenging me to be as Godly a person as I could be and she had given me a perfect moment to accept her challenge and be that good friend.

I guessed now was as good a time as any. I turned to face

the guys and said, "Henry, Richie, I have something important to share with you."

"What?" Henry asked.

"Tim's here!" I shouted.

It was true too. His dad's car was turning the corner onto our street and I could see Tim in the passenger seat.

Everyone turned around and saw Tim and the car.

"I thought he was gone for a week?" I said.

"Wow that went fast!" Henry said with a laugh.

We all got up and ran to meet the car as it pulled up in Tim's driveway.

"What are you doing home?" I asked as Tim got out of his car.

"Tim's got great news!" Mr. Phillips said proudly.

"Good and bad news." Tim said. He had a funny look on his face. Part happy and part sad all at the same time, if that was possible.

"Well, before you tell us, I have to tell you how awesome it was to see you on TV last night!" Richie said.

"Yeah, did you see us on the news?" I asked.

"Yeah, that was cool!" Tim said. "How are you feeling, Johnny. I'm totally sore all over! I'm kind of glad I didn't have to swim today after all."

"Man, I could barely get out of bed this morning!" I said. "But it's that good kind of sore though, do you know what I mean."

"Yeah"

"Hey, how come you didn't have to swim today? You're mom made it seem like this meet was a big deal or something."

"And what's this great news your dad mentioned?" Henry asked. "Do they want to make a movie of you and Johnny body surfing all the big waves in the world? That's it, isn't it! You're going to be famous! Hey, can I be an extra? I can be one of the guys in the background that says 'Whoa, dude!' when you wipeout or something. This will be great! We're going to travel the world! People will flock us for our autographs! When do we start filming? Will I need an agent? Do I get my own trailer?"

Henry, once again, had gone into one of his classic over the top moments. Richie grabbed him and put his hand over Henry's mouth to get him to be quiet.

"Easy, boy." said Richie. "Why don't we let Tim tell us what's up."

"Yeah, let's go sit down on the grass and I'll tell you. There's a lot."

We all went over and sat down. I had an uneasy feeling in my stomach by the way Tim was acting. He wasn't sad, just different. I looked at Summer with concern. She just looked at me and shrugged her shoulders. Even her amazing sixth sense couldn't pick up on what was going on in Tim's head.

Tim started in. "The swim meet I was going to this week was to try and qualify for the Olympic development team."

"The Real Olympics? The Olympic-Olympics?" Henry asked.

"Yeah those Olympics."

"Whoa!" we all said. "Awesome!"

"My dad had an Olympic trainer come up to him at my last meet and told my dad that he thought my time in the 100 freestyle was very close to, or might have even beat the record time in the United States for my age group and would I consider coming down to San Diego to swim for some of the mucky-muck coaches down there. My dad, obviously, said yes and that's where we went to this morning."

"Did you swim for the coaches already?" Summer asked.

"Dude, you're fast, but you can't be that fast!" Henry said. We all laughed.

"No, I never swam. When we got there I met the head of the Junior Olympic Development Team. He is in charge of finding all the young swimmers in the nation that are good and training them to possibly make the Olympics. I was scared just standing next to him. This guy was king. He called all the shots."

"So if he's the guy, why didn't you swim for him?" I asked.

Tim went on to tell us an amazing story about how, when he got there, most of the people already knew who he was and came over to shake his hand and say hello. He met one coach after another and got to tour the whole facility. They all knew him because Tim's coach had been sending film of Tim swimming in meets for the past year without telling anybody. Tim had broke the national record in his age group for the 100 freestyle about a year ago and when his coach saw that he knew Tim was fast, and possibly could be Olympic fast.

When Tim arrived, all the coaches knew him instantly because they had been watching Tim's films and they were already impressed with him; so impressed that some of them were already preparing how to train him. They had spotted slight flaws in his swimming stroke and knew if they could correct them, Tim might be able to swim even faster, if that was at all possible.

"So, I never had to swim for them. They just wanted to meet me and my dad in person to explain to us what the next steps were and ask me if I'd like to train with them."

"You said yes, Right?" I asked, knowing the answer. This was, of course, Timmer the Swimmer.

"Yes, I said yes! It took me all of about two seconds!"

"Way to go, Tim." Summer said. "You're going to be living your dream!"

"Do they have an Olympic cannonball team down there?" Henry asked. " I'd make that team easy! Maybe you could take them films of me doing my famous 'Girl Soaker XLT.'"

"Speaking of girls; are they hot?" Henry continued.

"I'm not sure about a cannonball team, but yes, there are girls, lots of girls, tan, good looking, and, most likely, only interested in swimming. There isn't a lot of time to do anything but train down there. It's serious stuff. I may only meet a girl when I look up to breathe while swimming laps."

"Oh, you'd be surprised how we girls watch you guys without you knowing it." Summer said as she glanced at me.

"I knew it!" said Henry.

"Hey, this sounds like all good news, Tim. In fact, it's better than good news, it is great news? What could possibly be your bad news?" Richie asked.

"Yeah, what's the bad news, Tim?" We all asked.

Tim went silent for a second and stared at the ground. Then he looked up and said, "I have to live down there to train. We're moving to San Diego."

Tim looked over at me to see my reaction. I didn't react. I

just sat there in disbelief. I couldn't believe what I had just heard. How was I going to make it through life now? How could I possibly live without Timmer the Swimmer nearby?

JOHNNY'S SURF FACT NO. 9
Good surf & Route 66 meet at the famous Santa Monica pier which boasts a ferris wheel and carousal.

CHAPTER nine:
"FISH OUT OF WATER"

For the next week I just walked around with a blank stare on my face. I made it to school and I think I ate food occasionally, but everything was pretty much a blur.

"How *was* I going to make it through the rest of my life without Tim around? Who was going to protect me? Who was going to get me through the rough times? Who was going to continue to challenge me to try new things? Who was going to put my life in peril on a weekly basis?"

These are the questions that I kept repeating in my head over and over again. Questions that I had no answers for. I guess I had just thought Tim and I would be friends and live across the street from each other forever. I was never much good at thinking too far ahead, except when Tim and I would strategically plan our summers together.

"What about summer? Who was going to help me plan the perfect summer? Most importantly, who would I share it with?"

I passed Tim in the hallway at school each day and each day I'd ask him the same question, "Still moving?"

He gave the same answer each time. The answer I knew he'd say. The answer I didn't want to hear.

"Maybe he'll decide not to be a swimmer." I thought to myself. "Kids our age change their minds all the time don't they?"

Of course, it was wishful thinking and I knew it. Tim

would be a fish out of water if he wasn't swimming, and so I'd muster up a smile and respond with a half-hearted, "Cool" each time he said, "Yes, still moving."

I would head out to my backyard each day when I got home and climb up on the decking of our swimming pool and just sit there staring at the water. I'd have my usual pity-party and think how boring swimming in the pool would be without Tim there to bring the latest swimming game or challenge. I was never going to know what "Pool Game Number Three" was.

I couldn't shake the sadness. I knew I had two other great friends in Henry and Richie, and that they could come up with enough cool things to do to fill a lifetime, but Tim was a different kind of friend, the kind I was pretty sure I needed and wanted to keep me from going crazy . . . and now he was leaving, so hello crazy.

Summer walked around the corner of my house and climbed up on the deck and sat down next to me. She obviously knew I was hurting inside.

"How are you doing, Johnny?" she asked, knowing I was bummed.

"I'm good." I said, trying to sound okay. She saw right through it.

"You've been walking around like a zombie the past couple of days. I mean more like a zombie than you usually do."

I laughed a bit out loud. Only Summer could say the right thing at the right time.

"You're not moving are you?" I asked. "I don't think I could handle that kind of a one-two punch."

"Nope. I'm not going anywhere. You're stuck with me, Johnny."

That didn't sound too bad, but it didn't make everything seem back to normal either.

"What are we going to do without Tim here, Summer?"

"I've been thinking about that." she said, "And I know what I'm going to do."

"Do tell." I said. "I can't come up with anything!"

"I'm going to do two things actually." She said. "The first thing I'm going to do is write down all the great times we shared together so I can look at them and laugh every time I miss him."

"That won't work. That's not like having him here!"

"Oh really, smarty pants!"

"What about the time when we were eight years old and you, me, Henry, Richie and Tim went to the swamp on old man Turner's farm and decided to play Huck Finn and Tom Sawyer. I'll never forget that day."

I had forgotten about that day. It was a classic moment in our lives. We had just finished watching "The Adventures of Tom Sawyer" that week in our English class at school and we decided to go to the swamp on Saturday, build a raft, and pretend to float down the Old Mississippi River. It didn't quite work out like we hoped it would, but it was hilarious and great fun just the same.

Tim was Huck Finn, because he was bigger and stronger than the rest of us. I was, of course, Tom Sawyer, Summer was Becky Thatcher, Henry made a great Injun Joe and Richie, well, Richie decided to be Mark Twain so he could record what happened for his book, and because we had run out of good characters for him to play.

We brought hammers and nails, rope and a couple of oars from Henry's dad's kayak. They were expensive oars and Henry repeated over and over that we had better not break them or lose them. We assured him that nothing like that would ever happen.

We knew there was some old wood near the shore of the swamp. It was left over pieces from the fencing that old man Turner had put up to try and keep kids off his farm and away from the swamp. It lasted about a day before kids had pulled it down and were enjoying the bike trails, tire swing and tree climbing again.

We still had to sneak onto his property to play at the swamp, but his house was so far away and there was a hill in the way, so he couldn't really see or hear what was going on unless he came to the swamp in person. Old man Turner was, as his name suggested, an old man, so making the trip to the swamp didn't happen very often. We would take our chances of him not showing up because the fun at the swamp always outweighed getting caught.

When we all got there that Saturday, some of the usual kids were there. Older kids were doing jumps with bikes off of ramps they had formed on the trails. Kids were climbing trees and taking turns swinging on the tire swing that was attached to the branch of a giant tree that hugged a cliff next to the swamp. Kids would climb in the tire and a friend or two would push them with all their might. You would actually swing out over the swamp, which was scary, and be high off the ground because of the cliff. Everyone wondered the same thing about the swing.

"What would happen if the rope broke right in the middle of your turn?"

That little bit of fear also added to the fun.

There were also a couple of kids fishing from the shore. No one had ever caught anything and we were actually pretty scared about what they might catch. No one really wanted to know what was down at the bottom of the swamp. Better to leave well enough alone we all thought. They mostly caught a patch of swamp moss or a piece of drift wood. We looked around at the group of people and as we began to get into character for our day of Tom Sawyer fun, we just thought of everyone as town's folk. Folk we'd never see again because we were going to build a raft and float away down river.

The four of us guys began to collect planks of wood and assemble them into a raft near the edge of the swamp. Summer "Becky Thatcher" did, well I don't know what she did. Maybe she gathered berries or something for the long trip ahead.

We hammered and tied the planks together with rope. Tim would jump up and down on it to test its strength.

"It be a mighty fine raft, Tom!" He said in his best Huck Finn voice.

"That it be, Huck!" I said and we all laughed.

"I'm not writing my book with grammar that bad" Richie said. He put a twig back in his mouth which he was using as a pipe and went back to pretending to write everything down.

We laughed again, but not as hard as when Henry attempted to say something like Injun Joe.

"Many moons we work on raft. Injun Joe tired, take nap,"

he said in the funniest accent we had ever heard, and then he plopped down on the raft and pretended to fall asleep.

We laughed so hard we couldn't work for a few minutes. I buckled over and had to kneel down I was laughing so hard. Tears came to my eyes, and when he snored, using the same accent, we all fell down laughing until we practically lost our breath. We pleaded with him to stop snoring, he was killing us. I was getting a side ache.

Summer came over when she saw us all on the ground laughing.

"Okay, what did I miss? What did you do, Henry?"

She knew who the culprit was. She knew who could take us all out with one humorous blow!

"I brought us berries for the trip." She said in a nice southern voice.

"Injun Joe, no like berries! Like pizza!" Henry said without looking up from the raft, and the laughter started all over again.

Somehow, eventually, we finally finished our raft, and it looked pretty good too. Not exactly like the raft from the movie, but not bad. The real question was not how did it look, but would it hold us all?

The four of us guys each grabbed a corner of the raft and began to walk it over to the water's edge. I could see that it was bowing a bit in the middle, we all saw it, but nobody said anything. We slid it out onto the water and hoped it wouldn't just keep going down to the bottom of the swamp. It didn't. It floated! It actually floated!

"All right!" I said, shouting out of character. I quickly changed back into Tom Sawyer mode. "I mean, there ain't a riverboat around got anything on our raft, right Huck?"

"Right Tom!" Tim said.

Tim knelt down and held one corner of the raft so it wouldn't sail away.

He looked up and said, "Okay, who's first?"

We all looked at each other as if to say, "Not me!"

Our lack of confidence in our water craft was showing.

"Ladies first!" Henry said, motioning to Summer to hop on board.

"A true Southern gentleman would go on ahead of me to make sure it was safe first."

Summer was as quick as she was smart. It was a great comeback to Henry's urging.

I happen to know there were no gentlemen like that in the area and we'd be standing around all day if something wasn't done quickly.

"Hey, Huck." I said. "Since you're the biggest and strongest kid I've ever knowd, maybe you should go first. If it holds you, it will sure-fire hold the rest of us!"

That not only made sense, it took me out of the loop for a second or two. Tim agreed and asked us to hold the raft while he tested it out. He stepped up hesitantly, one foot at a time until all his weight was on the raft. He worked his way to the middle. It was holding him up and it barely went down in the water either.

"All aboard!" He shouted, and one by one we gingerly stepped up on to the raft, checking its buoyancy with each person. Henry came last and as he climbed on he pushed with his back foot and we began to move away from the edge.

"The oars!" I shouted.

Henry looked back and saw that he had left them on the shore by accident. He immediately jumped back off to grab them, but his jump made the raft surge away from the shore and by the time he returned we were already six or seven feet off shore.

"Here, catch them and then you can row back and pick me up!"

"Okay." I said.

"Don't drop it!" He shouted as he threw the first one. I barely caught it and I got nervous because we were moving further and further away from Henry.

"Should we row back and pick up Henry and the other oar?"

"No, one oar will just make you go in a circle! Catch this one and then come back." Henry shouted.

Henry tossed the second one our direction, but missed us badly. The oar hit the water to our right and skidded ten feet away into the deeper part of the swamp and began to float away.

"Oh man!" Henry shouted.

"Don't worry, Henry." Tim said. "It will probably float to shore somewhere. Keep your eye on it."

It was floating all right, but not towards shore. It was drifting more towards the cliff where the tire swing was. There was no way to get to the water's edge there. We would have to row over towards it to try and grab it.

"It's floating to the deep end of the swamp!" Henry shouted. "You have got to get that oar, or I'm a dead man!"

"Give me the oar, Johnny." Tim said. "I'll row us to it."

I handed him the oar and he started rowing. Richie and I

knelt down and tried paddling with our hands. I don't think we were doing any good, but we kept trying.

Henry followed the oar from the shore to keep an eye on it and soon it was banging against the bottom of the cliff like I figured. Henry made some kids stop swinging on the tire swing so he could be right on top of it and point it out to us.

We were getting there, but it was taking forever. We were just creeping along but going in the right direction. It would only take a few more minutes and we'd have it. Henry felt relieved and a bit more relaxed. He also got bored and began to swing back and forth on the tire swing to kill time. He could also look down at the oar every time he swung out over the swamp.

We were within ten feet of the oar, and everything seemed to be working out fine. Our Mississippi River adventure would be back on track in a few minutes. We'd grab the oar, row back and pick up Henry and be off!

That, of course, was when everything went bad.

A loud snap, followed by a billowing scream, rang through the air above us.

Henry had swung out one last time on the tire swing and as he sailed out over the swamp, the rope on the swing finally broke. That was the snap we heard. The billowing scream was Henry falling toward the swamp and directly at us!

"Look out!" I yelled as Henry came falling in one direction and the old tire came falling in another. We had two obstacles to dodge!

The tire just missed Richie's head as it hit the water with a violent splash. Henry came next and, out of instinct, tucked himself into a cannonball position. When he hit the water the splash was probably some kind of a world record, but there was no reason to celebrate because when he landed he landed right on top of the oar floating below him. When the two of them came to the surface the oar was bent at a ninety degree angle. Not good.

The wave his dive made was not good either and it rocked our raft hard. We all tried to keep our balance, but as one of us stumbled, it was like a domino effect and one by one we all fell into the swamp.

Tim dove instead of jumping. He was a brave man to be going head first into the muck of this swamp. Richie seemed to actually get salute off like he was going down with the ship and I just slid off the edge trying not to have my head go under the water. It didn't work.

Summer, however, having lived a good life I guess, stood in the middle of the raft, handled the rocking and rolling and miraculously stayed on.

We all then swam over to the raft. There we were, four wet heads peaking up on each side of the raft and Summer in the middle just looking at us in silence and shaking her head.

"Tire swing, bad juju!" Henry said in his ridiculous accent, and we all busted up laughing.

"That's one of the Tim stories that I'm putting on my list." Summer said as she pushed me towards the pool. The slight rocking of my pool deck reminded me of the raft.

"Yeah, that one is a keeper. I can't believe I hadn't thought about it in a long time."

"I'll let you borrow my list of "Tim times" when I'm done, or better yet, write your own. I'm sure it will come in handy." she said.

Summer again showed she was too smart for her own age.

"Yeah, maybe I will!" I said. "Hey, you said you were going to do two things now that Tim was leaving to go train in San Diego. What's the second thing?"

"I'm going to cheer for him! I'm going to watch and see, and when he makes the Olympics, which I know he will, I'm going to be his biggest fan and cheer him on!"

"Hey, good idea Summer! If we follow his swimming career, it will seem like he's closer to us. Oh, and nice try, but I'm a closer friend to him, so I'll be his biggest fan, not you!"

"You're a closer friend?" She asked. "You know you might only have a few days to talk with him and prove it. You know, like we talked about before."

"Yeah, I know." I said. "Tim and I have done some serious planning together in the past; maybe it's time to do some serious planning for our future!"

Summer knew that I knew what she was talking about. We stood up and I thanked Summer for helping me, once again.

"Do we hug now or what?" I laughed.

"Sure!" she said, and she moved closer to me before I could tell her I was just kidding. She smiled, leaned over, and . . .shoved me into the pool, clothes and all!

"Man overboard!" she shouted as she climbed down the ladder and ran off laughing before I could splash her.

Tim would be missed, but with Henry, Richie and especially Summer, I'd never feel alone. Time to go find Tim and do some real planning!

JOHNNY'S SURF FACT NO. 10
Duke Kahanamoku is considered the
Father of Surfing. He introduced the
sport to mainland California in the 1920's.

CHAPTER TEN:
"GOING OUT WITH A SPLASH"

It was weird to see a For Sale sign on Tim's lawn. I sometimes would stare at it for hours from inside my house. Every time a realtor's car would pull up with possible buyers, I'd hope they'd not like it and move on. I was hoping that if everyone in the world interested in moving here showed up and didn't like their house, then they couldn't move and Tim would have to stay.

"It was time for another reality check!"

I realized that wasn't going to happen. The selling was inevitable, so instead, I began to study the people that got out of each car. Any one of these families might end up my new neighbor so I'd imagine what they were like just by seeing how they dressed and how they walked up to the house. I also, watched to see if there were any kids my age with them. That would be a crucial factor for the future.

"Was there another Tim out there?" I asked myself.

"No" was the answer every time.

There could never be another Tim out there. He was a one of kind friend.

Hey, there's a guy my age getting out of that car, a nice car too; maybe too nice. They all looked over dressed.

"Hey, there's no room for any rich, snotty people on our street!" I said to myself, having judged them before I'd even met them.

They'll move in and the first thing they'll do is build a

big, nice built in swimming pool in their backyard. The kind of pool you see in hotel brochures with the rock formations and waterfalls. It will have a spa that ten people can sit in and colored lights and a big platform for diving off.

Henry will become good friends with that kid and he won't want to come over to my house and swim anymore. He'll practice his world class cannonballs from their impressive platform that makes my pool's deck look like nothing.

Their family and Summer's family will become good friends and they will go with them on summer vacations together, instead of with us. They'll handle all the block parties; the cook outs and Fourth of July celebrations. They'll take over the entire neighborhood. Then they'll find something they don't like about us and start a petition to get us moved off the street! They'll buy our house for practically nothing, tear out our poor excuse for a swimming pool and have the house bulldozed just so they can put in a parking structure to handle all the cars, of all the people, coming over to party with them. They'll put a helicopter pad on the roof of it for when the President of the United States stops by to get advice on global affairs!! Then they'll go for world domination!!!!!!!

"Hey, Johnny, are you okay?" My mom said softly as she walked in my room. "You're face looks all angry."

"Uh, yeah, I'm fine." I said, trying to recover.

I guess my dad was right about my over imagination.

I still waited to see that family leave though so I could get a good look at their faces.

"You never know." I thought.

Wait. Speaking of Henry and world class cannonballs. I wonder where he is. I could use a little Henry time right now to cheer me up.

I called him on the phone and told him to get over to my house and make me laugh right away.

"Oh, and wear your swimsuit, my dad just cleaned the pool and it's filled to the brim with water!"

"Not for long!" Henry said.

I put on my trunks and grabbed something to eat, but not much. I didn't want to wait a half hour before swimming because I ate too much. I never really knew if that "cramping because you went in the pool to soon after eating" theory was true or not. I had never seen anyone cramp up and sink to the bottom of a pool before, but then again, no one dared go in too soon, so there was no way to test the theory. I could maybe eat a bunch of food and test it myself. I could challenge the myth and see if it was true or not.

"Nah!" better to leave well enough alone.

I barely got to the backyard myself before Henry and Richie came running in. Henry ran right past me and started up the ladder of the deck.

"Sorry it took us so long to get here, Johnny." Henry exclaimed as he climbed. "I was starving so I ate half a pizza before we left."

He then went right to the platform, leaped in the air and planted a cannonball to end all cannonballs right in the middle of the pool. The splash was so big that some of the water actually went over the fence and hit Summer's bedroom window.

Water also splashed over all sides of the pool and when it finally calmed a bit, the pool water level was down about three inches easy.

"That's my "El Cannonball Perfecto XLT!" Henry said. "What do you think?"

"Impressive!" I said.

Richie and I jumped in the pool and we laughed and played for about an hour. I learned two valuable lessons that day.

One: if Henry could eat half a pizza and go right in the pool without cramping, that old theory was back up for discussion. Too much quality pool time was being lost to kids everywhere for having to wait for a half hour to go by.

And two: that as long as I had these two clowns in my life, everything was going to be okay, Tim or no Tim.

Hey, watch my cannonball!" Richie said from the platform.

"Your cannonball?" Henry shouted. "You don't have enough meat on your bones for a good cannonball."

"I'm not using my weight, chubbo, I'm using science. I worked out a mathematical way to enter the pool and create thrust by the angle and speed at which I enter the water. It's all physics."

"It's all baloney!" Henry fired back.

"We'll see." Barked Richie and with that he checked the wind with his finger, moved a bit right on the platform and jumped.

Seeing his long skinny body curled up into a, well it wasn't a ball, but whatever it was it made us laugh before he even hit the water, and when he hit, it was an amazing sight.

At entry into the water, Richie went in without the water making a sound or even splashing at first. It was like suspended animation. Everything just seemed to freeze for a split second, then like a true cannon firing, a blast of water shot high in the air, higher than Henry's XLT, and not only hit Summer's window, it soaked it. It was awesome!

I looked over at Henry and he was just standing there with his mouth open. He couldn't speak.

"How'd I do?" Richie asked when he came back to the surface.

"Round one, science wins!" I said. "Back to the drawing board, Henry."

"This isn't over!" Henry said with confidence. "This moment has just inspired me to greatness. I have more work to do!"

"Yes you do, Henry!" came a call from Summer's house.

Summer had her window, her soaked window, open and was yelling down, but at the wrong soaker.

"The first little splash was okay, but soaking my whole window is too much, Henry!"

Henry tried to tell her it wasn't him, but he couldn't get a word in; not at first.

"You're going to come up here and clean the outside of my window and never splash up here again. Do you read me?"

"But it wasn't me, it was Richie!" Henry pleaded.

"Nice try, Henry, nice try. I know who thinks he's the cannonball king!" She continued her assault on him. "And you're through soaking all the girls at the City Pool for that matter."

"No, really Summer, it wasn't me!"

"Wow, trying to get out of it is one thing, but trying to have your friend take the fall for you shows what kind of a friend you really are, Henry!" She continued.

"You should probably sit down with them, Johnny, and tell them what a true friend is really like. They obviously don't know!" And with that she slammed her window shut.

"I've never seen Summer that upset have you, Johnny?" asked Richie.

"Yeah, you know her best. Is she going to kill me later? Do I really have to clean her windows?"

"No Henry, you won't have to clean her windows, and no she's not even mad at you, she's upset with me."

"Wait a minute. She chews me up and spits me out, when she should really be mad at Richie, and you say it's because she's mad at you?" Henry said, totally confused.

"Yep, you've got it!" I said.

"Got what?" Henry cried. "My head hurts, and I'm starting to cramp up!"

"That's the pizza." Richie said.

I decided not to go into the cramping thing. I knew what Summer was doing. She was letting me know, in her clever little way, that this would be a great time to talk with Henry and Richie about my faith. She was reminding me of the *good friend* I needed to be to these guys, and plan not only my life with them here, but also, where we were going when we left, and not just left the neighborhood like Tim, but when we left this earth.

I told the guys to sit down, I had something important to talk about, but before I could start, I was interrupted by Tim walking up.

"I could hear a world class cannonball fired from all the way over at my house." Tim said. "Is there any room on the deck for me?"

"Was the first cannonball or the second one louder? I have to know!" Henry asked.

"Let it go, Henry!" I said.

Tim climbed up and we all sat in a circle. Henry described his cannonball and then Richie's and Summer's reaction and we all laughed at Henry getting busted for not doing it. It was a great moment. A moment I wanted to last forever, but I knew wouldn't. Tim confirmed that with his next words.

"We sold the house!" He said.

It caught me off guard. It was way too soon for me to hear that.

"You didn't sell it to that snobby, rich family did you?" I blurted out.

"Who?" Tim asked.

"Never mind!" I said.

We all took turns telling Tim we'd miss him.

"Hey, what was that important thing you wanted to tell us, Johnny?" Richie asked. "You're not moving too, are you?"

"Maybe he made the Olympic Nose Picking Team and has to move to New Jersey to train," Henry said with a laugh.

We all laughed.

"No, I just wanted to tell you something I've been meaning to tell you for a longtime now and have been putting it off." I said.

I went on to tell them about why I got up on every Sunday and went to church. I shared that I didn't just go because my parents made me or wanted me to go. I told them I went because I had met a friend there; a true friend. The friend of all friends, and his name was Jesus.

I shared why He was my friend and how He proved his friendship to me by dying on a cross for me. I reminded them that the baby they see every Christmas in mangers on yards throughout the neighborhood and city grew to be a man and a friend like no other.

As my boldness in speaking to the guys grew I went on to tell them that Jesus was the most important friend they could ever have, and that when we die, we now have the chance to live forever because of Him conquering death and raising from the dead. I told them that I wasn't perfect, but in his eyes, every time I ask for forgiveness for the times I really mess up, He wipes my slate clean and makes me look perfect to God his Father, and that someday I'll get to stand in front of them both and have them call me friend.

When I was done, there was just silence. I glanced up at Summer's window and could see her looking out but trying not to be spotted. She was wiping tears from her eyes and I knew they weren't tears of sadness, but instead, tears of joy because I was finally being a true friend. A *wave of courage* had swept over me and I was being a true friend.

Tim was the first to speak.

"Wow!" he said. "I'm glad you told me that before I took off for San Diego! What if I never met anyone down there that liked me enough to tell me what you just did?"

"And why did you wait so long to tell us?" Richie asked.

I knew that question was coming eventually, and I also knew I didn't have a good answer.

"I know why." Henry said, which surprised me.

"It's not something you just say without thinking. It's too powerful! It needs planning and going over. It's like perfecting the perfect cannonball. You think about it, you study, you practice in secret and then you wait. You wait for just the right moment. You get all your friends around and then you jump! You jump with all your might so that when you land everyone feels its impact! Right Johnny! That's why you waited until now, right! It was the perfect moment."

It was the most profound thing I had ever heard come out of Henry's or any twelve-year-old person's mouth. I wanted to say yes, that his analogy was right on. I wanted to, and I was tempted to, but that would have been a lie. This was a time for truth and honesty.

"I wish that was the case Henry. I wish that was true and maybe, in God's timing, that's why I waited until now. But the real reason is I had put other things ahead of what was really important. I had made up excuse after excuse. I was more worried about planning summers and vacations than I was about planning our eternity together. I was being your friend just not being a really good friend, until now. Do you forgive me?"

"No, absolutely not!" Henry said. "You're not getting off that easy!"

"What do I have to do?" I asked in panic.

Henry could come up with some wild things to make you do in times like this and this was a doozey!

"You need to invite us to church so we can meet this Jesus friend of yours!" He said.

"Yeah, if we like Him he's one of us!"

139

"You'll like him!" I said.

"What about you, Tim?" I asked. "Want to join us at church this Sunday?"

"Hmmm. I could probably pencil you in, I guess. I'll have to check with my agent, I'm going to be a world class Olympian you know!"

We laughed and then threw rafts and anything we could find on the deck at him.

"Man and to think, I was going follow your career and actually cheer for you!" I said jokingly.

"You better!" He said. "I'm going to need all the friends I can get! San Diego won't be easy!"

I didn't like being reminded he was leaving, and soon. I knew it was going to change the neighborhood and my life forever. I figured my loss was someone's gain down there though. Some kid who never tried doing anything because he was too afraid was about to meet the guy that could build your courage like no one I had ever met; except for maybe the incredibly smart girl that lived next door.

I looked up at the window and motioned for her to come and join us.

As Summer made her way over I thought about how proud she'd be of me – that I finally rode the "Wave of Courage" it took to finally invite my friends to church and learn about the kind of friend Jesus wanted to be for each of them.

Maybe I did have what it takes to truly be a great friend.

"All right, enough talk!" Richie shouted. "Let's hit the pool!"

"Yeah, show me one of those world class cannonballs I've been hearing about, Henry." Tim said.

"Uh, you might want to talk to Richie about that." Henry said humbly.

"No." Richie fired back. "He's still the king. My cannonball days are over!"

Henry gave him a high five and headed for the platform. Summer came running in with her suit on, climbed the ladder, went up on the platform, pushed Henry out of the way and yelled, "Cannonball!" in a high, shrieking girl's voice and then jumped.

She barely made a splash when she hit the water and we all laughed until we all fell over.

"What?" she asked when she came to the surface. "Didn't I make a splash?"

"You always make a splash, Summer." I said out loud, not meaning to.

"Oooh!" Tim and Richie said, looking at me.

Henry broke the awkwardness of the moment by mimicking Summer's attempt at a cannonball, shrieking voice and all. Tim, Richie and I jumped in and a splash fight broke out.

Then Tim said, "Okay, everyone to the middle of the pool. Pool Game Number Three!"

"Uh-oh! Here we go again!"

THE END
(. . . but wait thirty minutes first!)

Did You Know There Was a National Day of Evangelism?

P.RŌJECT

Announces...
DARE TO CARE DAY
MARCH 16th

Sign Up Today!
Join with Other Believers!
Share Jesus One Friend at a Time!

www.project316.org

Project316 is an Internet-based, outreach ministry that encourages and challenges all followers of Jesus to share the salvation message found in John 3:16 with at least one person or more on or before March 16th-"Dare To Care Day," The National Day of Evangelism.

For More information Visit Our Website www.project316.org or Contact Us at info@keithpoletiek.com

Contact Founder Keith Poletiek at 951.201.2611 for Booking Information

Books by Keith Poletiek
"Johnny Lazarus in The Legend of Frog Finger"
"Johnny Lazarus in Vinnie's Steal Attempt"

Books by Keith Poletiek (Available Soon)
"Prayer of H.O.P.E. Outreach Training Guide"
"The Guardian Six – Genesis"

Ministries of Keith Poletiek
"Project316"
Learn an easy and effective way to share the gospel
message found in John 3:16 with at least one person
each year through Keith's online ministry
www.project316.org

"Dare To Care Day, March 16th"
Help spread the news that there is a new and
important day of the year for all believers
March 16th, Dare to Care Day. Learn how you can get
involved at *www.project316.org*
The concept is simple: Share 316 by 316
ONE LORD, ONE FAITH, ONE MESSAGE
ONE DAY, ONE PERSON AT A TIME!

Contact Keith for speaking engagements by email at
keith@keithpoletiek.com or by phone at 951.201.2611

Follow Keith's ministry and get more info about
Dare To Care Day at www.project316.org, FacebookTM,
TwitterTM and *keithpoletiek.com*

Keith Poletiek

For the past 25 years, Keith Poletiek has been traveling the nation sharing the Good News of Jesus in his own unique style to all ages. His zany humor, amazing word pictures, memorable stories and illustrations make Keith a favorite among those who hear him.

Keith's hit-home style of speaking brings the message of salvation to youth and families in a way that is clear and long-lasting. Keith will make you laugh and cry, but most of all, make you think and reflect on your life. Keith's passion is to see all people inherit the Kingdom of God.

Keith worked in Youth Ministry for four years before beginning his nation-wide speaking ministry. He was educated in Youth Ministry at Pacific Christian College (Now Hope International University) in Fullerton, California.

Keith is the founder of Project316 & "Dare To Care Day" (a national web-based outreach ministry), the author of *The Adventures of Johnny Lazarus Book Series* and *The Prayer of H.O.P.E. Training Guide (The Official Outreach Training Manual for Kids)*, Graphic Artist, Cartoonist (Creator of the Syndicated Cartoon Strip *Dude and Dude* seen daily on Comics.com, Screenwriter for Wide Open Productions, as well as the Marketing Director for Angeles Crest Christian Camp in the San Gabriel Mountains.

71325331R00082

Made in the USA
San Bernardino, CA
15 March 2018